Of Curses and Beauty

Elle Backenstoe

OF CURSES & BEAUTY

Cover design: Hannah Sternjakob

Editing: Jessica at Gwyn Edits

Line Edits and Proofreading: Colby Bettley at Novel & Noted

To anyone who has ever wanted
to run away to the forest.

There is danger in beauty
in the way that it beckons,
demanding to be witnessed,
captured, admired, held, possessed.

It's the painter's masterpiece,
the soprano's aria.
It is the day's splendid end,
the rose begging to be plucked.

But for all the world's beauty,
it stands to be remembered
that roses, though alluring,
are more vicious for their thorns.

CHAPTER 1

Alaine

A laine felt the stares of those around her like rays of sunlight as she strolled through her quaint village. She could bask in the warm caress of a few, but the eyes of many quickly turned to burning glares that chafed her skin, making her uncomfortable despite the crisp, autumn breeze. Hoping to stave off the worst, she gathered the edges of her cloak to her chest and buried her face deeper into the book she was reading.

It was, therefore, the fault of the gawking townspeople—and definitely not her preoccupation with reading—that led her to collide with the last person she ever wanted to see.

Lord Henrik Baxter's meaty hands had already reached out to steady her before Alaine recovered from the interruption. With all the grace of a startled chicken, she jumped out of his grasp, tripping on her skirts in her haste to avoid his touch. She hit the ground with a thud that she heard as much as felt, the sudden impact sending a shock up her spine that left her momentarily stunned.

As luck would have it, her temporary immobility provided ample time for Baxter to scoop her up, his hands taking too many liberties in his attempts to dust the dirt off of her.

Alaine had been far too young when she started to capture the attention of the men in her village. Her father called her beautiful with a smile that implied it was a blessing, but the women around town spat it behind her back like the curse that it was. In no time, she'd become simultaneously desirable and unwanted.

Men coveted her, but she had no friends; those she'd grown up with having shunned her when she needed them most. Even at home, she was not so naive to miss the green tinge of jealousy that had crept into her own mother's eyes whenever she looked her way.

It was a surreal experience to be a child one day and a woman the next. It seemed, at least to Alaine, that her body had made that leap before the rest of her, forcing her into a role with consequences for which she hadn't been prepared.

Surreptitious glances had turned into hungry stares. Casual touches had become statements of possession. Men flocked to her door, but no one stood by her side.

She was to be seen and not heard. Beautifully silent. An accessory and nothing more.

A *prize*.

Thinking about the number of times she'd been told to smile made her blood boil.

Now that she was officially *of age*—an arbitrary age that was surely determined by men, if for no other reason than because nothing in the world was ever determined by women—Alaine found herself constantly fending off offers of courtship and marriage proposals. Many of which were from Lord Henrik Baxter himself.

"Ms. Martan, you really must be more careful," Baxter spoke to her décolletage, ignoring all pretense of eye contact as she disentangled herself from his roaming hands.

Alaine bent down to retrieve her book that had fallen after the impact. The cover had been dirtied, but none of the pages appeared damaged as she flipped through them. She took her time assessing the condition of the book until it was clear that Baxter had no intention of moving on without acknowledgment from her.

A sigh of frustration escaped her as she straightened, smoothing down her skirts and returning the book to its position as a protective barrier against her chest. Her eyes lifted to find Baxter's cold blue gaze fixated on her. The hunger reflected there made her take an involuntary step back.

She angled her head and dipped into a curtsy in an effort to cover her hasty retreat. "Your pardon, Lord Baxter. I'm afraid I didn't see you there."

One corner of his mouth tipped up in an infuriating smirk. "No, Ms. Martan," he said, glancing pointedly at her book, "I suppose you wouldn't have. Bit of a hazardous hobby you've got there."

Alaine forced her lips to form a smile. If it more closely resembled a grimace, Baxter did not comment.

She'd heard many of the women in town tittering about Lord Baxter's supposed good looks. She suspected if you knew nothing about the man within, his facial symmetry and healthy physique would qualify for what most consider attractive. And yes, his nearly black hair and blue eyes were rare enough to be considered special in their small town. That, combined with the wealth of his family's estate, made him one of the most desirable bachelors in the village.

But it would take more than money and looks to win her hand. Alaine knew she was just another trophy for him to collect. Unfortunately, her refusals only served to entice this hunter further.

"I have spoken to your father." His hushed tone suggested his proposals were not public knowledge.

"He did mention that, as I recall," Alaine hedged. Baxter would have numerous reasons for speaking with her father, who was the most celebrated jeweler in town. Though she knew he referred to his most recent offer of marriage, she preferred to be wildly indirect when it came to discussing such matters.

"Yes, well," Baxter stepped closer, casting furtive glances as though we were discussing war crimes and not marriage. "He implied that *you* are to have the final say in your betrothal." His accompanying sneer told her all she needed to know about his opinion on the matter.

"Oh yes, indeed." She nodded fervently and placed the back of her hand against her brow. "I don't know how I shall ever endeavor to make such an important decision with my simple, feminine brain. What's a poor girl to do without a man to decide her life choices?" She didn't attempt to mask the sarcasm that dripped off every word.

For a moment, nothing but the wind passed between them. The evidence of her fierce spirit always gave him pause. He hated it, viewing her strong will as her one and only flaw. She could see it in his eyes, the way he wanted to break it—break *her*—and mold her into something more pliable.

As seconds became minutes of stilted silence, she assumed their discussion concluded and moved to step around Lord Baxter, only for him to sidestep directly into her path. She drew up short but refused to back down, craning her neck to meet his penetrating gaze with one of her own.

"Is it your lack of dowry which causes your resistance?" he asked. Though his tone hinted at curiosity, the words were intended to humiliate her. Recent difficulties had hit her family hard, and it was common knowledge that she'd be wed with little in the way of a dowry to offer her husband. "My family's lands provide well enough for me to forfeit my right to a dowry if it will sway your mind."

"I shall take that into consideration, Lord Baxter. Good day." She gave him a closed-lip smile but knew it didn't reach her eyes. Alaine had just about reached the limits of her propriety when she moved to leave a second time.

Her exhale of relief morphed into a gasp of shock as she was whipped around like a dog on a leash. With a vice-like grip on her arm, Baxter slammed her against the stone wall of the nearest building.

The coppery tang of blood filled her mouth as a throbbing pain blossomed across the back of her head. Though her vision swam from the impact, Alaine could feel the heat of his breath searing her cheek as he pressed into her space.

Rough stone bit at her soft flesh as she tried and failed to disappear into the wall behind her. She scanned the streets around them, desperate for help, looking for any way to escape the terrifying man who held her.

The village that had been bustling only minutes earlier was now quiet. The few people she could see turned their heads away, offering her nothing. She expected no less when all this village had ever given her were cold shoulders and leering eyes.

Baxter took hold of her chin with deceptively soft fingers, so at odds with the punishing grip around her arm that she flinched at its gentleness. A hot tear escaped the corner of her eye as he forced her to look at him. She cursed that tear and any sign of weakness that she bore to this man, knowing they would be used against her.

"I have been a patient man, Alaine, but I will not continue to tolerate these childish games of yours. When I want something, it is only a matter of time before I get it."

His gaze raked over her from head to toe. A sensation like a thousand spiders skittered over her skin and she shuddered. Though fully clothed, she had never felt more violated than in that moment when his eyes lingered on her curves. If she could, she would crawl into a hole, emerging only once her beauty had faded and Henrik Baxter had no more use for her.

"I will have you," he growled through clenched teeth. "This is your final chance to decide the terms before I stop asking nicely."

With a grunt, he shook her once—hard and jarring—the motion stealing the breath from her chest. Fearing another attack, Alaine squeezed her eyes shut as he drew back. Her lungs burned as she waited for the next blow to land. When none came, she cracked one eye open.

Baxter had gone.

At her instant relief, air flooded her lungs in heaving gasps. Though welcome, her respite was short-lived. The streets were once again occupied, the villagers having abandoned their hiding places in the calm following the storm. Some huddled in small groups whispering. Others stared at her outright.

Recovering her wits, Alaine bid her heartbeat to slow as she stepped away from the wall. Wrangling her panting breaths into a semblance of composure took more effort than she wanted to admit, but she pressed her lips together and forced deep, even breaths through her nose. She refused to look at her throbbing arm and arranged her cloak to hide the blossoming evidence of Baxter's attention. A bead of moisture slipped down her cheek. She didn't know if it was perspiration or the remainder of the tears she'd been holding back, but she swiped it away with the back of her hand, unwilling to let these hateful people see her shaken. Their actions thoroughly disgusted her and she felt ashamed for hoping there was even one kind soul among them.

With confidence she didn't feel but had plenty of practice faking, she lifted her chin, squared her shoulders, tucked her book beneath her arm, and strode away. She made sure to meet the eye of each person she passed, allowing all her venom and accusation to shine through.

Never had she felt more abandoned in her own town.

Only when stone walls became open fields did Alaine allow her tears to fall. They were silent, angry tears. Tears of mourning as she grieved the loss of the life she'd never live. She wanted to rage. She wanted to run. She wanted to open her book, step into the pages, and live forever in a world of happily-ever-afters.

A choked sound escaped her, halfway between a laugh and a sob. Real life was nothing like the fairytales she loved so much. It was only a matter of time before her responsibilities caught up to her. Courting. Marriage. She'd been lucky to escape them for this long.

When the dirt path forked before her, she hesitated. Only one path led home, but inside her was a growing desire to walk a different road. Somehow she knew the choice she made would determine more than just the direction of her feet.

To the east, lay her family, her duty, her past. But to the west, the tranquil forest beckoned her heavy heart. She knew what choice the heroines of her stories would make, but the question remained—would she find what she sought in the forest beyond, or would it prove yet another disappointment to heap on her shoulders?

At that moment, she preferred the safety of not knowing to the potential disillusionment of stepping into the forest and discovering she was not the heroine in her own story. If that made her a coward, so be it. She didn't have an enchanted sword or a fairy godmother. She was in this alone and if she knew one thing, it was that lone women garnered no favor in the real world.

CHAPTER 2

Daric

P rince Daric Halverson was not faring well. He squinted
against the sun as it crested the trees of his glade, cursing
its warmth as he panted from exertion. Sweat dripped from
every pore. It drenched his hair and impeded his grip on the axe
held at his side. He glanced at the pile of wood beside him, more
than enough to last him through the next several weeks, though
he knew he'd be back at it again tomorrow.

Deciding he was finished for the day, Daric let the axe slide
from his grasp and topple into the grass below. He plucked up
his shirt from where it lay discarded and used it to wipe the
sweat from his brow and neck.

When his stomach rumbled, he debated ignoring it, unwilling to surrender any bit of daylight to being indoors. Especially
in that dreadful cottage. Just glancing toward the offending
structure where he resided was enough to put him in a foul
mood. Its magical properties did little to sway his opinion in
the other direction.

Over the years, Daric had come to resent the small, enchanted
cottage that caged him, its stone walls reminiscent, yet wholly
different, from the castle he'd once called home. Within, he
couldn't help feeling trapped. Though the boundaries of his

imprisonment truly extended to the rotting wood fence that encircled the cottage, it was only under the thatched roof that his skin crawled with the overwhelming need to escape.

For centuries, he'd had no human interaction beyond infrequent visits from the witch who had cursed him to this solitary existence. Being confined to a cottage in the woods and the small plot of land around it played tricks on his mind. Some days he teetered on the brink of insanity, the emotional toll almost as great as the havoc wrought upon his fortitude.

Physically, he hadn't aged a day—hadn't changed *at all*. Even the length of his hair remained the same as the day he'd arrived. Inside though, he felt ancient, withered, and beaten down by time, a contrast to the strange reflection he saw in the mirror of a young man. A young man who no longer existed.

In the early years of his curse, he'd raged, violently and viciously. He was angry at the world, the witch, but mostly, at himself, for becoming ensnared so easily. Each failed escape attempt marked his soul in a way he knew was beyond repair. By the time he gave up trying, he was a shell of the prince he'd once been.

After ten years, he gave up hope of rescue as well.

When one hundred years had come and gone, he realized that everyone he'd known had passed on. Everyone who had possibly loved him, missed him, and mourned him, was gone. His mother and father, his friends and guards, he'd outlived them all. For whatever reason, it was that thought, and not his years of isolation, that made him feel truly alone. And after three hundred years of it, he'd all but lost his mind.

The man he had been had a reason to wake up each morning and push through every obstacle. That man had hope for the kingdom he would have ruled and the queen he'd find to stand at his side.

Now, all of those things were out of reach. He'd had one wish beyond being a good king, but in isolation, he had no hope of breaking the curse or finding the love for which he desperately yearned.

Like a caged beast, he worked constantly against the mounting frustrations that threatened to overtake him. Idleness was his enemy. He pushed his desires to the back of his mind, executing the same menial tasks day in and day out to keep from losing himself entirely.

Every day he woke, ate, cut wood, ate again, then slept. Rarely did he deviate from the choreographed steps of his clockwork dance, careful to maintain the ruse of living.

Whenever he stumbled toward the edge of madness, one thought kept him from plunging headfirst into the abyss—revenge.

As though conjured by his dark thoughts, the hunched figure of the crone appeared beyond the fence. Even the wind held its breath as the wicked creature beckoned him with a clawed finger. While logic begged him to stand his ground, anger propelled his legs forward toward the target of his vengeance.

He stopped as he neared the fence post, the witch wisely remaining out of reach. "What in the skies do you want?" he rasped. His voice, though unaccustomed to conversation, traveled easily in the now quiet forest.

The witch bared her teeth in the semblance of a smile and he braced himself for what was to come. "The time has come, Prince. Today, you will be a free man." Her hand uncurled, palm up in silent request. "You need only take my hand and I will remove you from this cursed place."

Daric regarded the proffered hand skeptically.

"Well, come on, boy," she snapped. "I haven't got all day."

With a sigh, Daric braced one hand on an upright and swung himself over the fence. It was low enough that he didn't have to put much effort into the jump. He landed lightly in the soft grass, but when he looked up, he found he hadn't made it to the other side. As always, his feet remained firmly within the boundaries of his curse. The cottage mocked him where it stood, before rather than behind him.

A cackle erupted at his back and he turned to see the witch doubled over with laughter, pressing a hand to her middle as her face became an unflattering shade of puce. With a fresh burst of fury, Daric stormed back toward the cottage only to be halted, spun, and held in place by invisible hands.

The witch's touch disgusted him.

He made several attempts to shake off the phantom hands, his body trembling from the effort, but it was no use. Unable to move so much as a toe, he clenched his jaw and waited for the hag's laughter to subside.

Minutes passed before the witch finally straightened, wiping a tear from her eye as she sighed in contentment. "That will never get old."

Daric willed his eyes to say all that he could not. If he had even an ounce of magic, he'd fight back. As it was, he could do nothing but wait until she decided she was done with him. With any luck, she would soon tire and leave.

"As much as I enjoy our little visits, Prince, I've actually come with some news." With unnatural speed, she plucked a falling leaf out of the air and tucked it into the folds of her cloak.

Daric blinked, confusion and surprise battling within him as the witch continued speaking as though nothing was amiss.

Navigating the witch's moods was like trying to dodge rain-drops in a storm. No matter how hard he tried, she always managed to throw him off-kilter.

"We are expecting company."

If he hadn't already been completely immobile, Daric would have frozen at the proclamation. His eyes flicked to the witch, begging the old woman to read his mind and answer all the questions he had.

Who? Why? Why now?

The witch acknowledged his questioning gaze with another sneer. "Be ready, Prince."

Her laughter remained long after she'd faded away to noth-ing. Daric swore if he ever got free of this place, he'd strangle the life from that witch with his bare hands.

CHAPTER 3

Alaine

A laine knew she'd made the wrong choice the second she walked through the door of her family's modest, two-story home. Her mother and father sat facing each other at opposite ends of the dining table, entrenched in conversation which ceased abruptly as she entered. When their heads snapped to her in perfect unison, they looked like a pair of guilty school children caught doing something wrong. She almost chuckled, but the despair on her mother's face, coupled with the pity on her father's, froze her laughter in her throat.

A draft followed her inside the house. It stalked beside her, stealing the warmth from her fingertips and dancing ice-cold claws up her neck. She shivered as much with cold as a premonition. Her unease lingered as she bolted the door closed and rushed to her parents.

"What's happened?" Alaine asked, checking first for any other signs that something was amiss. Nothing else in the house appeared to be out of order, but the looks on her parents' faces suggested bad news.

She hoped there hadn't been another death in the family. The recent passing of her paternal grandfather had come as a terrible shock to her family and they were still feeling the effects several months later.

Her father scrubbed a hand down his face while her mother rose to wrap her in a tight embrace—an act wholly out of character that set Alaine's teeth on edge.

The cloying scent of patchouli and clove clung to her mother like a second skin. Alaine detested the fragrant oil that her mother frequently applied. There was no reigning in the cough that dispersed some of the powder from her mother's hair in a cloud of fine dust.

Alaine pulled away, both overwhelmed by her mother's nearness and desperate for answers. Though she tried to put distance between them, her mother's hands continued to linger on her shoulders, a solid weight likely intended to comfort her, but it only added to the mounting pressure already stacked there.

"It would seem your grandfather had some substantial debts when he passed." Alaine could hear the quavering in her father's voice though he spoke from across the room, still seated at the dining table. He pressed his shaking hands to the solid wood, throat bobbing as he swallowed once. Twice. "And so the responsibility falls upon this family to settle the debts owed."

Tears pooled in her mother's eyes as Alaine met her gaze.

"I don't understand." Her eyes flicked back and forth between her parents. "How much do we owe? Surely, with the coming holiday, you'll have commissions coming in. I saw a small group gathered to admire Lady Faraday's new necklace. I'm sure they'll all be flocking for something equally amazing."

Her father shifted in his seat, looking everywhere but at her. "Unfortunately, the sum is far more than our meager earnings could cover. The debt is so long-standing that it has been called due in three months' time. We would be bankrupt."

She gasped, unwilling to accept the truth of what her father said. They would lose everything; not only the money, of which she cared little, but his business, their possessions, and their home.

Her thoughts churned as she grasped for a solution. There had to be options available to them. Surely, her parents would not accept bankruptcy so quickly. She nodded, as though reassuring herself. Her father still wouldn't look at her, but she refused to smother the kernel of hope that flared in her chest. "What can I do?" She didn't have much, but she would gladly sell everything she owned to help her family.

Seeking aid, she turned beseeching eyes on her mother whose guarded expression gave Alaine pause. If there was more bad news, she wasn't sure she could handle it.

Her mother, sensing Alaine's distress, offered her a half smile that she didn't return. "Lord Baxter has generously offered to settle the debt in exchange for your hand in marriage."

The words took time to hit their mark and she stared in silence until they struck true. The quiet stretched as Alaine experienced every emotion from shock to rage.

At the age of eight, she'd fallen through thin ice while playing with friends. She'd screamed as she plunged until the freezing water stole her breath. She recognized the sensation now, the feeling of helplessness as her lungs seized, knowing the chance for rescue was slim and fading.

The chiming of the grandfather clock called her back to the present, but she couldn't shake the anxiety that quickened the blood in her veins. Her hands shook with the restless need to do something—anything—demanding that she move.

She speared her father with a glare that conveyed her full disappointment at this betrayal. He winced at the anger she directed at him and raised both hands in mock surrender.

"You cannot mean to marry me off to that man to settle a debt. You know him. You know what kind of man he is. You told me I'd have a choice." Her voice came out strangled and she struggled to breathe around the lump in her throat. "We can figure this out. We'll get the money another way. There are other wealthy families with eligible bachelors. Just let me think. I'll pick someone before the week is out!" She was rambling, but she didn't care. She refused to be sold like cattle, to Henrik Baxter of all people.

Alaine felt the world tilt as her legs crumpled beneath her. She sank to the floor, her mother unable to support her weight as she collapsed into her. Fabric pooled around her, a tranquil sea of blue that mocked her rising panic. She forced herself to take a deep inhale and closed her eyes as she blew out the breath. Her parents said nothing as she worked to calm her racing pulse.

There were ways out of this nightmare. There had to be.

Her mother patted her back and Alaine fought the urge to slap her hand away, burying her anger as she always did.

"Don't pout, Alaine, you'll wrinkle. You could do worse than Lord Baxter," said her mother, a hint of disdain in her voice. "Not all men have the resources and wealth of a family like that. He's not bad to look at either," she whispered conspiratorially.

Her father cleared his throat, but Alaine refused to look at him. "Baxter has graciously given us until the first snowfall to make our decision. I will stall as long as I can, but as of now, he is the best hope we have of making the deadline."

She nodded in acknowledgment that she had heard him, but she was through letting others dictate her life. There was nothing in this world that could make her want to marry Baxter. She would find another way to save her family.

"I am sorry, Alaine."

She didn't acknowledge her father's apology or her mother's stoic calm as she dusted herself off and walked out the door. Though her heart begged her to slam it, she gently pulled the door shut until the latch caught. The damage was done. No good would come from her throwing a fit.

The sun greeted her as she walked outside, the cheerful light a slap in the face after such a bleak conversation.

No one called after her.

No one chased her.

They knew she'd do this for them. It was an easy sacrifice to make—her freedom for their security—and the time had come. She'd been running from her duties for too long and now it was too late. Had she accepted one of the other offers for her hand earlier, she wouldn't be facing the prospect of marrying Baxter now. She knew without a doubt that he would attempt to sabotage any chance she had of finding another suitor. If it came down to it, she would do what she needed to do to save her family, but she would exhaust every other possibility before that day came.

For now, she needed to clear her head. She needed to strategize. Most of all, she needed to get away from other people. This time when she came to the fork in the road, she turned toward the forest. Just this once, she told herself, she'd follow her heart. Just once, before she surrendered to expectations.

Chapter 4

The Witch

Deep within the forest, prowled an ancient being of great power. They were known by many names and had inhabited many bodies—Their own having been long since lost to time. It was pure chance that They came to possess the body of a young enchantress, Eudora. A fool who had attempted a spell beyond her abilities. She would have died if it weren't for Their efforts.

There are reasons one should not meddle in affairs of the heart. Most cannot afford the cost demanded by such magic, this witch included. When her life force reached out for the strength to complete the task, They had answered.

And now They waited.

In another cottage, far from where the prince remained caged, the Ancient One bided Their time. The centuries ticked by in a haze of potion-making and spell-casting, broken only by Their frequent visits to the prince, and the hunt for the other; the one who would complete the curse.

Time had meant nothing in Their greater form. However, in this mortal skin, They felt its passing like the rusting of metal, feeding off Their energy even as They extended Eudora's life far beyond human standards.

Regardless, Their time in this body was nearing its end.

It had been a whim—a mere curiosity—that saw this Ancient One answering the call of one so seemingly insignificant. They'd been drawn to the chaos, the spectacle, the desperation. They'd danced to the ridiculous melody of the impossible and dared to make it possible.

Their primordial, potent magic—Their very entity—had twined with the witch's, morphing the spell and permanently altering the course of events. In doing so, They had saved the witch from a fatal error, but They also had inadvertently cursed them all.

The spell, though mutated from its original form, still required the same result—something near impossible to achieve. It weighed Them down like iron chains, demanding near-constant energy to keep from being suffocated.

Surely, these inconsequential tidings were above such a powerful creature. And yet, They remained.

Perhaps They did not wish for it all to have been in vain. Or perhaps some small part of Them remembered what a powerful thing it was to love and be loved.

Whatever the reason, They were determined to see this through, no matter the outcome.

And now, all the players were set in motion. If this chance was missed, They wouldn't have another. Even now, Their energy flagged—the cost of maintaining too many threads. They had maybe another year before They'd need to abandon all to their fates. A year before They couldn't hold on any longer.

They feared it might already be too late for the prince. That he'd shown any hint of fire during Their earlier visit was promising, but only time would tell if it was enough. Mortals were not meant to endure for so long, particularly under such trying conditions.

A tingling sensation crept over Their hands, stilling the knife They wielded in midair. The rat squirming in Their grasp let out a series of squeaks as sparks lit at Their fingertips. The frightened creature slipped from Their clutches and scurried away to freedom as They were momentarily distracted by the lightning arcing from finger to finger.

The Ancient One had expected this particular sign much earlier, but the girl had possessed a stronger will than They'd anticipated. Not many could ignore Their summons for so long. Indeed, this girl had proved far more difficult to procure than the prince.

Hurrying to the witch's scrying mirror, They upended the cauldron and toppled several stacks of books in the process. Even after centuries of wearing this skin, They were still acclimating to the clumsy way it moved, so unlike Their natural grace. The constant bruises marring the witch's pale flesh were a nuisance, but one They quickly forgot as They reached the spelled glass.

The dark mirror swirled to life as They approached, revealing an area of the forest with far fewer trees and more sunlight. A young woman stepped into view. Her fellow humans had deemed her beautiful beyond compare, but They had selected her for an entirely different reason.

This curse was about to become far more interesting. Now, with the final piece on the board, the witch's spell that was centuries in the making was finally nearing fruition. It was just as well, for They tired of the prince's endless melancholy. Watching him had become a tedious bore and They hoped the girl would provide some entertainment at the very least.

They donned the witch's cloak, reverting to her original form, that of the red-haired maiden, before stalking into the forest to hunt Their quarry. If all went well, They'd have the girl by nightfall.

CHAPTER 5

Alaine

T he forest welcomed Alaine with the calming harmony of birdsong and rustling leaves. Sunlight pierced through the trees in muted rays, casting the scene in a peaceful glow. Her shoulders eased as she inhaled the scent of fresh pine and earthy loam. Though she'd escaped the probing eyes of the townspeople and the weighty expectations of her parents, the strain continued to linger as she breached the tree line. Safe within the confines of the forest, she urged the stress of her obligations to melt away, kicking off her shoes to curl her toes in the soft moss beneath her feet. She'd nearly forgotten the book that was still clutched in her hands like a shield. Her stiff fingers resisted as she freed it from their clutches, gently laying it beside her shoes so she could carry on unburdened.

For a while, she only walked, enjoying the forest for the reprieve it offered. Meandering through the trees reminded her of playing in the forest as a child, brandishing long sticks like swords and battling imaginary foes.

Once, Alaine had vowed to always be the hero in her own story. Considering Henrik Baxter's proposal seemed like a betrayal of that promise. She didn't know if she could survive becoming that awful man's wife. Acceptance would be a sacrifice of everything she valued in herself. She'd be a stranger to her own eyes.

Before he had offered to clear their debt, she'd known no redeeming qualities of the man. It couldn't be chance that he was the one coming forward as their savior now. She should have demanded details about the debts. The timing was too suspicious and her father too trusting for this to be a mere co-incidence. She'd bet anything that Baxter was the one behind this mysterious debt, perfectly setting himself up to swoop in and save the day. If he thought this ploy would have her running into his arms, he had to be out of his mind.

Not for the first time, Alaine considered taking away that which made her so desirable. She could cut off her hair, hide her body beneath ill-fitting clothes, or even scar her face if it came down to it. The option had always lurked in the dark recesses of her mind, but altering her appearance felt like admitting defeat. *She* was not the one who needed to change.

"I wish there was another way out of this," she mused aloud, tapping her lip thoughtfully.

A snapping branch froze her in place. Her breath hitched as she swiveled and caught a glimpse of a dark shape darting be-hind a thick, moss-covered trunk. In her mindless wandering, she had failed to notice the silence that had descended upon the forest. Now that her ears strained for any sign of life, she heard nothing. No birds sang. No critters scurried about. Even the air was stagnant with no breeze to stir the leaves above.

"Hello? Is someone there?" Her voice trembled, but she cast about for something, anything she could use as a weapon. She found a sturdy branch and held it out, her body quickly falling back into her old playtime habits.

Her bare feet were quiet on the leaf-strewn forest floor. Still, she took care placing her feet as she crept toward the offending tree. It occurred to her that she may be sneaking up on a wild animal. Her instincts screamed at her to run away, but she was almost certain the figure she'd spied had been human.

She allowed herself one steadying breath and rounded the trunk, branch raised to strike and a battle cry on her lips, but there was nothing there.

She turned in a circle, certain she was going mad, but there was nothing to suggest anyone had been there.

With a huff, she tossed aside her makeshift weapon. The beginnings of a headache bloomed behind her eyes and she pinched the bridge of her nose, closing her eyes against the pain.

The forest remained eerily quiet and she couldn't shake the feeling that she was being watched.

Confused, weary, and more than a little on edge, Alaine decided it was time to head home. Unfortunately, she no longer knew which direction would lead her there. Each tree looked as unfamiliar as the last, each stone as unremarkable. She tried to remember what angle the sun had been at when she'd entered, but her memory was a blur.

Her heartbeat began to quicken as nervous energy flooded her. Her fingers twined together, feet moving of their own volition. Unwilling to risk moving deeper into the forest, she paced the small clearing like a caged animal.

Back and forth.

To and fro.

She worried her bottom lip between her teeth as she wracked her brain. The forest lay to the north and west of the village. She had no idea if she'd traveled south at all, but she could put her back to the sun and follow her shadow to the east, provided she had enough daylight to make it home. Though if she had wandered south, she could pass by her hometown of Maribonne and never even know she'd missed it.

"Are you lost, dear?"

The voice that broke through her building hysteria was soft and kind, but it couldn't temper the scream that tore from Alaine's throat when she glanced up to find a woman standing less than a stone's throw from her. It took a moment for the woman's words to register through the haze of shock, but once they did she had to fight back waves of embarrassment.

The woman regarded her with the patient eyes of a mother, though she appeared little older than Alaine herself. She wore a simple dress of homespun and a rich-looking, black velvet cape that contrasted with her free-flowing auburn locks and pale skin. She was a picture of incongruences, at once alluring and foreboding.

Nevertheless, she might be the only chance Alaine had of finding her way home before dark.

"Yes," Alaine's voice was barely a whisper. She cleared her throat and tried again. "I do appear to have lost my way."

The stranger's smile grew, and for a moment Alaine could swear she saw a completely different face staring back at her. The image of a withered old crone vanished as quickly as it had appeared and Alaine suspected her anxiety was making her see things that weren't there.

The woman held out her hand. "I can help you." Her voice was a gentle caress that promised safe passage and true intentions.

Alaine didn't know how a voice could express so much in so few words, but her feet moved of their own volition toward the woman. In the blink of an eye, she was standing before the woman, fingers outstretched to clasp the proffered hand. She hesitated with her hand barely hovering over the woman's upturned palm. Something itched at the back of her mind, a feeling that this woman, like her choice to enter the forest, was about to change her life forever.

She shook her head. If it wasn't the anxiety, it was her wild imagination concocting these strange ideas. There was no magic at work here. This wasn't her fairy godmother, come to solve all of her problems. Alaine had not been chosen by fate to meet a handsome prince and be carried away to his castle. No. This was just a kindly woman from a neighboring village—or perhaps the forest itself—offering to help her find her way home.

Alaine took a deep breath and joined their hands.

The air *whooshed* from her lungs as the forest disappeared into a cloud of white smoke like a scene from a dream. Wind rushed past them, their cloaks and hair billowing up around them. Alaine's stomach dropped and she swore her feet left the ground as she tightened her grip on the stranger's hand.

If it weren't for the bite of fingernails against her skin, Alaine would have sworn she was hallucinating. Exhilaration bubbled up inside of her, forcing a giddy laugh to escape before she had the chance to contain it. Embracing the feeling, she threw her head back and closed her eyes, reveling in the freeing feeling of weightlessness.

All too soon, a shift in the air alerted Alaine to their descent. She squinted but could make out nothing beyond the woman's fiery hair. Even the sun failed to penetrate the swirling mists around them.

Her feet met solid ground, sending a jolt through her body at the impact. She had the vague impression that she should be afraid, but she felt only awe as she turned in place, watching as the smoke cleared to reveal an unfamiliar stone cottage with a thatched roof and simple fence. They were still deep within the forest, surrounded on all sides by oaks, aspens, and evergreens, the foliage so dense it was clear they were far from any village.

"This isn't my home," she said with a sad smile, for she knew if given the chance, she would gladly remain here for the rest of her days. It was exactly the kind of picturesque refuge she escaped to in her daydreams.

When no response came from the mysterious woman, Alaine tore her gaze from the enchanting scene and found herself alone again.

She squeezed her eyes shut, certain this was all some twisted dream. Surely, Baxter had jostled her harder than she realized. She was hallucinating. That was the only plausible explanation for this bizarre turn of events.

With her eyes closed, she noticed a return of the tranquil forest sounds; birds chirping, leaves rustling, and above it all, the steady sound of someone chopping wood.

Alaine said a silent prayer to whoever was listening and hoped that this new stranger would prove more helpful than the last.

Still barefoot, she raced toward the sound, nimbly leaping over fallen branches and ducking between fence posts. She slowed as she reached the cottage and crept around the back where the fence line continued, encircling several trees. The rhythmic *swish* and *thunk* grew louder as she rounded the corner and spied a man swinging the ax. He faced away from her as he chopped, his bare back rippling with the movement. A linen shirt lay tossed aside and the breeches he wore did little to hide the impressive figure beneath. He was easily the largest man she had ever seen.

The skin on her arm prickled, and she remembered the bite of Baxter's grip on her flesh. Nibbling on her bottom lip, she considered her limited options. There was no telling what part of the woods she currently occupied. If she set out on her own again, she'd likely never find her way back home.

Still, she had to swallow down a lump of fear before announcing her presence. Stepping forward tentatively, she lifted her chin and cleared her throat.

The man stiffened but did not turn. Instead, he reached for another log to cleave. *Was he ignoring her?*

She took another small step. She was close enough now to see the sweat tracing lines down his muscled back. "Excuse me!" she called.

The man whirled in a blur of motion that sent sweat flying in all directions. Alaine took a step back as wild eyes found her across the too-short distance. She suddenly wished she'd picked up another stick before confronting him.

He crossed the distance between them in three long strides. When he raised a hand as though to reach for her, Alaine flinched away. His eyes darkened at her reaction, but he didn't try to touch her again. Instead, he ran his hand through his loose, wavy locks, pushing them back from his face as his gaze flicked around nervously.

"Are you real?" he whispered. His voice was gravelly like he didn't speak often, which considering he lived in a secluded cottage in the woods, was probably accurate.

His question took her aback. "I... Yes, I'm real," she stuttered, suddenly unsure of her own existence. "Are you?"

He laughed, a jaded, sarcastic sound that was more bark than anything. "Oh, I'm real alright."

"Alright," she repeated, dragging out the last syllable. "Well, I was hoping you might be able to help me find my way home. I am from the village." She gesticulated behind her, though she wasn't sure exactly which direction her village lay in. The man didn't appear to be listening anyway as he continued to look anywhere but at her. "See, I was out for a stroll through the forest and I'm afraid I got a little turned around. I thought this woman was going to help me, but she just brought me—"

"What woman? What did she look like?" His focus snapped to her, shocking her again with the intensity of his gaze.

She bristled slightly at the interruption, but described the odd woman to him, making sure to mention all her strange contradictions. His eyes lit with recognition as she spoke. Her voice trailed off when it came to the magic. She didn't need him thinking she was delusional.

"That meddling witch," he muttered, then turned and shouted into the trees. "Playing matchmaker now, are you? Well, you can't just toss me any homely lass you find wandering through the woods. I've got standards to uphold! No offense meant."

He tossed the last bit over his shoulder in such an off-handed way it took Alaine a moment to realize he was referring to her.

"I beg your pardon. Homely?" No one had ever referred to her as anything but stunning, beautiful, at the very least *pretty*. She told herself not to take offense. This was what she wanted after all, for someone to see her as something other than a beautiful girl. No matter how hard she tried she couldn't shake off the sting of that word—homely. Perhaps it hurt because she was still being seen at only face value. Even in the forest, her attractiveness was her only worth.

Crestfallen, Alaine started to back away from the peculiar man who continued to berate the trees. When he failed to notice her departure, she angled toward the cottage and stopped short at the sight before her. Illuminated by the faint rays of the sun, she caught her reflection in a darkened window, but the face that stared back was not her own.

The changes were small, nearly insignificant when considered individually, but the picture in its entirety was one of a stranger. The slightly larger nose slashed straight down rather than turning up at the end. The eyes, though the same shade of brown, were ringed by dark circles like she hadn't slept in days. Her hair had lost its luster, and her skin was duller by comparison. The healthy flush that usually graced her cheeks had faded into an unforgiving pallor. Overall, the effect was not disgusting, but rather unremarkable. Homely, she supposed.

"What was it you needed?" Alaine hadn't noticed the man turning his attention to her, but when he spoke she found his reflection in the glass. He studied her with open curiosity, head tilted to one side and hands planted on his hips.

Though she tensed at having her back turned to the man, he didn't appear to be ogling her backside. In fact, her eyes briefly met his as she scanned his face, but her focus kept being pulled to more interesting parts of his body. Alaine had never been in a situation that provided her with such an ample view of the male form.

The word *beast* flitted across her mind as the perfect summation of his heavily muscled physique and untamed mannerisms. He wasn't handsome in the classical sense, in the way that village girls would fawn over, but he possessed a kind of animal magnetism. A wildness that called to something primal inside of her. Somehow, she got the sense that he could be both fiercely loyal and incredibly passionate. A forgotten part of her longed to be on the receiving end of either.

She tore her gaze from his sculpted form, feeling heat creeping up her neck. She fumbled with the ties of her cloak and cleared her throat. "I'm searching for my way home, if you think you might be of any assistance."

"And where is this *home?*" He spoke the word with such maliciousness that Alaine turned to face him, suddenly unsure if she could trust him at her back.

She swallowed as she considered the wisdom of sharing the information with a stranger. Unfortunately, she knew she couldn't find her way home on her own. She would have to rely on someone. "I'm from the village beyond the woods—Maribonne. My family lives on the outskirts."

"I've never heard of this Maribonne. What is it you're running from?"

"I—who said I was running from anything?" She winced as she realized how defensive she sounded.

"You can't have ended up here by chance. You're either running from something, or searching for something. Which is it?"

"I'm *here* because an insufferable witch dumped me here when I thought she was offering me aid. I'm *searching* for my way home and I'm *running* out of patience." She huffed out a breath, turning back to the window as she crossed her arms in indignation. Her breath came fast and shallow, though she knew there was no reason to get worked up. She would find her way home and everything would be fine, but she needed this man's help and that required her cooperation. She took a deep breath in and released it slowly, a technique she'd often used when dealing with the village men.

"I suppose you may have a point," she conceded.

He tilted his head toward her reflection, but didn't speak.

She didn't know why, but she felt the sudden urge to share her story with this stranger, to rid herself of this burden to someone she'd never have to see again. Perhaps it was the way he looked at her without judgment, but staring at his reflection, she could almost believe he was a figment of her imagination. A knight in shining armor, though he looked anything but. Alaine knew better than most not to judge by outward appearances alone.

"It's a bit of a funny story. This isn't actually my face. I mean, it is, sort of, but I'm truly—well, uhm—pretty. Ugh, that's not right. I mean, it is, but it makes me sound conceited. What I mean to say is that everyone else thinks I'm pretty. In my village, they sometimes call me Beauty." *Why was this so uncomfortable?*

She took another steadying breath, determined to get this off her chest. "All my life, I've been made to believe that only my beauty makes me worthy. Worthy of attention, worthy of affection, worthy of marriage. I guess you could say I'm running from my beauty and searching for my true value. Apparently, I'm halfway there. Though that's really only half the story." A smile graced her face, but his remained unmoving, contemplative. "Why did you make your home here? Are you running or searching?"

"I'm cursed," he replied with a shrug. "This isn't my home; it's my prison." He glanced away, crossing his arms over his chest and reminding her that he wore little in the way of clothing.

"Right. Well, I really should be going. My father will be missing me terribly."

His answering laugh sent shivers down her spine.

"I don't think you understand. You can't leave."

She whirled, breath catching on a gasp as she half expected him to disappear into a cloud of smoke and leave her here alone forever.

"What do you mean I can't leave?" The words ran together as they wheezed out of her, high-pitched and breathy.

"I mean that in all the time that I've been here, I have yet to find a way out, but by all means, do try." He stepped aside with a flourish. "Perhaps it will be different for you."

It wasn't true. It *couldn't* be true.

Alaine ran.

When she reached the nearest fence post, she tossed decorum aside, throwing one leg over like a man mounting a horse. She slid off the other side and landed in a heap of skirts. Frowning, she picked herself up. She'd expected some kind of magical barrier or guard. Surely, it couldn't be that easy. She turned, looking back to see if the beastly man had followed her, intent to keep her hostage, but there was no man, no cottage before her.

Now she knew she truly was losing her mind.

"Well, it was worth a try."

Her heart leaped into her throat at the sound of his voice coming from behind her. She swiveled to face the man, finding him just as he had been when she'd vaulted the fence, except instead of being on opposite sides, it was like she had never tried to leave. The look on his face told her the result would be the same if she tried again.

All at once, the events of the day came crashing down upon her shoulders. Her limbs grew heavy and her thoughts became foggy. As much as she desired to be free of this place, she could not muster the energy to exhaust every possible means of escape, especially if they were all as futile as this one had been.

"How long have you been stuck here?" She dreaded the answer but feared the unknown more.

He leveled his intense stare at her and she saw the answer reflected in his eyes—all the lifetimes he'd witnessed, unchanging and alone. It was too late to recant her question and, though she braced herself in anticipation of the coming blow, nothing could have prepared her for the truth.

"Three hundred and eleven years."

CHAPTER 6

Daric

Daric had forgotten what it was like to interact with another person. His only conversations in recent years had been with the witch that had cursed him. He'd seen far too much of *her*, though she was oddly absent since delivering the girl to his woodland cage.

His feet dragged as he made his way to the fence post where her crumpled form lay. She had fainted upon hearing the length of his solitude. He was loath to move her, knowing it would set into motion whatever schemes the old witch had cooked up, but it wouldn't do to leave her laying in the grass. There was no telling how long it would take her to recover and he wouldn't have her waking alone and scared.

He squinted as he stood over her, trying and failing to see her for the beauty she claimed to be, not that it mattered to him. He'd had countless beautiful women throwing themselves at his feet in his life before the curse. It didn't satisfy him then and was of no consequence now. Though, she did pique his interest.

With a sigh, he scooped up the poor girl, ignoring the way her gentle curves nestled into the hard planes of his body. She seemed young, younger even than he had been when he'd first been cursed. He tried not to think about the loved ones she'd unwittingly left behind, the father she'd mentioned. She still had so much life left to live and now it was lost. Lost to some stupid curse on the whim of a witch.

He couldn't pity her without feeling sorry for himself in the process, so he focused on how this would change his life for the better. It was too much to hope for meaningful conversations and companionship, but he would be grateful to share his space with another person.

As he reached the door, he commanded the cottage to open it. The girl didn't stir as it swung open on quiet hinges. It took longer than he expected to safely maneuver himself and the girl through.

Daric turned to shut the door and caught sight of the familiar old crone standing on the other side of the fence. Her hood hung low over her face, but there was no mistaking the wicked smile she cast his way. Glaring in return, he shifted the girl just enough to make a vulgar gesture in the witch's direction and slammed the door closed on her responding cackle.

Chapter 7

Alaine

A laine didn't remember passing out or being carried into the cottage. Even though she woke to the calming crackle and warmth of a fire in the hearth, her body shook uncontrollably. Somehow, she had still believed she would wake to find it had all been some bizarre dream resulting from her blow to the head or the stress of her potential engagement.

Shaking off the last remnants of unconsciousness, she pushed herself up to sitting. Her head throbbed in protest, but she welcomed the distraction. She didn't want to think about what the beast had told her. If she'd wanted to change her circumstances, she had certainly succeeded. At least now she couldn't marry that brute, Baxter. He wouldn't want her anyway, not now she was stripped of the one thing he prized. The thought was a small consolation, but it brought a smile to her lips nonetheless.

"Feeling better, then?"

Alaine jumped at the sound of his voice. For such a large man, the beast was remarkably quiet. She imagined that it was a result of all the years of solitude; there would be no reason to make any noise if all he could hear was the sound of his own footsteps.

"As good as can be expected," she responded meekly, pressing back into the plush sofa like she could disappear into it.

The beast had donned his shirt, but the thin material did little to disguise his sculpted chest and wide shoulders. His dark blond hair had been pulled back as well, accentuating a square jaw that was dusted with stubble. Somehow, she had failed to notice the startling amber shade of his eyes. Now with his focus intently on her, it seemed impossible to ignore.

Though this man had shown her no interest, the memory of Baxter's possessive hands was still too raw for her to be completely at ease being alone with him in such close quarters. She knew a woman didn't have to be beautiful for a man to take her to his bed. It had to be doubly true for a man who had spent over three hundred years alone.

He stepped forward and she flinched away. Once again, his eyes narrowed at her reaction, but he only lifted his hands toward her. It was then that she noticed the steaming teacup he was offering. She felt like the worst kind of person as she nodded in acceptance, silently berating herself for making hasty judgments against this man who, so far, had only helped her.

She took a tentative sip of the tea and was pleased to discover her favorite; lemongrass and lavender, sweetened with just a touch of honey.

"It's delicious. Thank you," she said in an attempt to recover from her earlier blunder.

He settled himself into a large, wingback armchair across from her and leaned back, filling the space with his impressive frame.

Alaine took the time to study her new housemate. He appeared more at ease than he had upon their first meeting. Between his brows, a small crease had formed, but his jaw held none of the tension from earlier. A large, gold ring glinted off one finger as he spun it absently. Alaine thought it a remarkable treasure for such a humble life. Perhaps it was a clue to his past, but she tucked the information away for now.

She guessed that he had as much to wrap his mind around as she did. After so long alone, taking in a permanent guest must be a huge change.

"I'm Alaine." She figured she should be the one to start introductions given she had more recently spent time in social settings. "Alaine Martan."

In response, he heaved out a sigh and scrubbed his hand down his face. "Daric. Just Daric."

She had no intention of pestering him about his family name since it was clear he didn't want to share it, or perhaps couldn't remember.

"I'm terribly sorry for intruding on your solitude. I can assure you it was not my intent, *Just Daric*."

One corner of his mouth twitched towards a smile. "You'll have to forgive my lack of social graces, Ms. Martan. I assure you I harbor no ill will toward you. It will be refreshing to have some company after all this time."

His words bespoke a familiarity with social etiquette, one she did not expect to find in a man who appeared so undomesticated, but she knew better than to judge a book for its cover.

"Just Alaine would be fine."

She smiled kindly and sipped her tea, at a loss for how to continue in this awkward situation. She'd been trying to escape what would be a loveless marriage, and now here she was, forced to *live* with a complete stranger. The irony was not lost on her.

"The cottage is enchanted." His voice was warmer than it had been earlier. Though it still retained a rough, gravelly edge that suggested disuse, she found the deep timbre calming.

She followed his gaze around the room, noting the details she'd missed when she'd first awoken. The space was clean, though sparse. Gray stone walls were offset by warm wooden timbers. A sink and cupboard stood along the wall by a small dining table, the extent of the furniture in that room. There were no personal effects, though the herbs hanging to dry along the hearth helped it feel more lived-in. A large rug covered much of the floor, its color faded from apparent age. In fact, every textile in the room—the armchair, the sofa, the curtains—seemed a pale reminder of what Alaine imagined it had once been.

The same might be said of the man that resided there, she thought, bringing her focus back to him.

"You need only ask for something and it shall be done. Food, hot water, firewood, clothing. It has already added a bedroom for you there," he said, gesturing to one of the doors that branched off the main living space.

He seemed fit to leave it at that, but she had endless questions threatening to burst from her lips. She settled for the most pressing.

"Is there truly no way to escape?"

"Are you so eager to return to your provincial life? Or is it your *beauty* that you desperately want returned?"

The bite in his words startled her. "Actually, I'd be happy to return to my life as you see me," she responded with equal venom. For all the reasons she had to return to her life, her beauty was the least of her concerns.

His gaze didn't burn as he considered her, but she felt it nonetheless like he was trying to pull back all her layers and uncover what lay beneath. Though she wore another face, Alaine felt more seen under his scrutiny than she ever had. She hugged her arms tight to her body to counter her discomfort.

Leaning forward, Daric rested his elbows on his thighs and threaded his fingers together. "We have been cursed. We will remain at this cottage, unchanged, as the world moves on around us. We will be trapped until we meet the terms that will break the spell."

"And?" she prompted, scooting to the edge of her seat. "What terms would those be?"

"If only it were that easy," he said with a dark chuckle. "I cannot speak of my own, but I suspect yours has something to do with determining your self-worth without the mask of your beauty."

She opened her mouth, then shut it and promptly opened it again, gaping like a fish. This man was breaking down every preconceived notion she had of him. She looked at him again with fresh eyes. He was rugged in every sense of the word, with long, barely-tamed hair, impressive musculature, and calloused hands. But she could see the hints of nobility in his posture, the way he lifted his chin and pressed his shoulders back. She wondered what secrets his past held, but refrained from probing for the time being. It was intrusive enough having to stay in his home—or prison, she supposed. It wouldn't do for her to pry into his personal life as well.

"Let me see if I'm understanding all this correctly. You've been cursed for over three hundred years and you've yet to find a way free of it?" He nodded solemnly. "So, all I need to do is find a way to free myself from this curse before my family grows old and dies."

"That about sums it up."

"Piece of cake." She jumped as a large piece of chocolate cake appeared on the low table between them.

Daric chuckled, the sound rich and intoxicating.

"It would seem the cottage is on your side," he said, pointing to the cake. "Are you hungry?"

She knew she should eat, but her stomach churned from the chaos of the day and she didn't think she could handle adding anything more to it.

"No, thank you. I think I need to lie down again."

She set her teacup aside and rose to retire. Daric stood as well, forcing her to crane her neck to look up at him. The cottage wasn't large by any means, and his presence overwhelmed the cozy space. Alaine thought she should feel intimidated, but instead felt oddly safe with this beast of a man.

"It is unfortunate circumstances that have brought us together," she said, "but I think I am glad to have met you, Daric. I can think of no man besides my own father with whom I would rather be forced to cohabitate."

Daric laughed; a real laugh this time, not one of his humorless chuckles. "I'm honored, Beauty."

She rolled her eyes and headed for the room he'd indicated as hers. "Good night, Beast."

CHAPTER 8

Daric

S leep eluded Daric as his thoughts continued to revolve around his strange new guest. Alaine was like no one he'd met before—at least, no one he could remember. His memories grew hazy the more time passed.

She had made him laugh and that was a feat in itself. More to the point, she seemed to genuinely like him with no notion of who he was or the title he held.

Used to hold, he reminded himself.

He had no idea if Alaine would be the one to break his curse, but he thought he wouldn't mind spending eternity with her if it came down to it. At least, it appealed more to him than eternal solitude.

Whatever the witch was thinking by bringing her here, it didn't bode well for either of them. For all he knew, Alaine could be a puppet sent to torment him, to give him hope where he'd had none, and then crush it like a bug underfoot.

It was possible but seemed unlikely. Unless Alaine was a better actor than he could ever guess, he suspected she was as much a pawn in this game as he. That didn't mean she was his ally, though.

When the first rays of the sun began to peek through his bedroom window, he gave up chasing sleep and rolled out of bed. He pulled on the closest pair of breeches before stepping out his door, surprised to find Alaine already seated at the table, a hearty buffet before her.

She glanced at him as he walked over and immediately averted her eyes, a hint of pink rising to her cheeks. That seemed odd. She hadn't appeared shy the night prior, but Daric figured late-night conversations with a stranger must seem far more intimate when remembered in the cold light of dawn.

"Good morning," he said, hoping to break the ice that appeared to have reformed overnight.

She cleared her throat before returning the sentiment, eyes downcast.

"Is there something wrong?" *Had he done something? Did he have something on his face?* He swiped a palm over his face for good measure. His hair was sure to be a mess, but that was a common occurrence hardly worthy of such avoidance.

"Oh! No. Forgive me," Alaine stammered. "I'm not accustomed to seeing men in such a state of undress."

He glanced down to see that he was in fact only half dressed, a state which had mattered little in the last few hundred years.

"Ah, of course. Pardon me. A shirt, if you please." He addressed the last bit to the cottage itself, which provided a simple tunic that he pulled on quickly. "Better?"

Her eyes flicked to him as though afraid to subject them to too much skin. Upon seeing him fully dressed, she exhaled in relief, a shy smile appearing between her still-ruddy cheeks.

"Sorry—"

He halted her with a raised hand before she could finish. "There's no need to apologize. I've spent too long away from the rest of the world. Please excuse me if I forget myself from time to time." He gestured to the spread before them, eager to change the subject. "This is quite the feast."

She ducked her head, brushing a lock of hair behind her ear.

"I didn't know how specific I needed to be with my request. I just asked for some breakfast." A nervous laugh escaped her and Daric smiled in response.

"It must be showing off for you then. Whenever I ask for breakfast, I'm lucky if I get toast." As if to prove a point, a small plate of slightly burnt toast landed in front of him.

Laughter burst from them both and he marveled at how quickly he had come to feel at ease with this woman. Perhaps it was the lack of social construct, but he suspected he would enjoy Alaine's company, even if he'd met her in the rigid confinement of the court.

She leaned forward as he took the seat across from her, curiosity crinkling the edges of her eyes. He was surprised to find himself curious about her in return. Who was this self-proclaimed former beauty who'd been caged with the beast? What had she done that warranted being cursed alongside him?

Thinking of the curse reminded him of the witch and his mood soured. In the end, his mistrust of the witch won out against his desire to learn more about Alaine and he held his tongue, taking a large bite of dry toast instead.

Seeing her in the morning light, he found he deeply regretted his hasty assessment of her appearance the day before. His angry words had been for the witch and Alaine had gotten caught in the crosshairs, an innocent victim to his rage. She wasn't beautiful by any stretch of the word, but neither was she homely. She had kind eyes that shone with intelligence, and a strong jaw that, when thrust forward in a bout of stubbornness, could almost be considered cute. He took another bite before any of the words in his head could escape. The last thing this woman needed was his judgment.

All this time, she observed him. He could see the questions dancing on the edge of her upturned lips, but she waited—albeit impatiently—until he finished his meager meal. He had nothing against talking during meals, but found he rather enjoyed watching her squirm. If there was one thing he had learned in over three hundred years of cursed solitude, it was patience. He didn't even try to hold back his laughter as she practically vibrated with excitement while he washed down his last bite with a gulp of water.

"Go on," he said, still chuckling. "Ask away. I know you want to."

Alaine laughed.

He liked her laugh, liked how she didn't try to hide it behind her hand or wrestle it into something dainty and polite. Her whole body laughed and it made him feel lighter than he had felt in years.

"Well, I know you can't speak about your curse, so will you tell me what you can about yourself?" She fidgeted with her fingers, twisting her hands together as she spoke. "I tossed and turned all night, thinking about how I was sharing a roof with a man who is practically a stranger."

At the mention of Alaine lying in bed, Daric was reminded how long it had been since he'd last shared a bed with a woman. He hadn't thought about *that* in a long time and he refused to give consideration to the idea now. He shifted uncomfortably, aware of Alaine's eyes upon him. Inexplicably, he felt some measure of comfort knowing they had both lay awake, thinking of the other. This situation had to be as surreal to her as it was to him—likely more so.

Alaine rushed to fill the silence that had stretched too long. "What I mean to say is, you don't have to share every intimate detail of your past life, but I would be grateful for anything that would help me know you better." She smiled nervously. "I would be happy to reciprocate, of course."

Daric nodded and leaned back in his chair, scratching the stubble on his chin as he stalled for time. *What could he share about himself?* His life here was not a life at all. And his life before? He wasn't sure how much of that he wanted her to know. That he was a prince of a land that no longer existed? That he'd been haunted by the thought of entering a loveless marriage, much like she had? That he'd had women literally begging to make them his queen before they knew a single thing about him?

No. Some things needed to stay buried.

"A truth for a truth?" he asked.

Her shoulders dropped as she loosed a breath. "Sure."

He took a moment to consider his three hundred and thirty-four years, before deciding the best opening truth. Placing one forearm on the table, he pitched forward for dramatic effect. She instantly mirrored him, angling toward him as though they were sharing intimate secrets.

"I *hate* hats."

Her eyes widened for a split second before she burst out laughing again. He grinned, satisfied that he'd reduced her to another fit of giggles.

"I'm sorry," she said, wiping a tear from her cheek. "You what?"

"I hate hats. I've never been able to find one that fits just right. I have a rather large and impressive head, you see."

"Yes, I can tell that you do have a rather inflated head."

He cast her a sidelong glance and she pulled her lips between her teeth to contain the laughter that still shook her shoulders. His cheeks hurt and he knew he was using muscles that hadn't seen much use in recent centuries. He waited for her to settle then gave her a pointed look, raising his eyebrows to indicate it was her turn to share a truth.

"I don't know if I can top that." She bit her lip as she cast her glance around. "Oh!" She leaned forward, mimicking his earlier movement, a wicked gleam in her eyes. "I can wiggle my ears."

With a flourish, she tucked her hair behind her ears, lifted her chin, and folded her hands on the table. He watched with rapt fascination as her gently curved ears moved the tiniest bit and back again, over and over.

"Will wonders never cease?" he said with mock sarcasm. He grinned and she returned it, and just like that, he found the hope he thought he'd lost long ago.

CHAPTER 9

Alaine

T hey exchanged truths for what had to be hours if the sun's position in the sky was any indication, but she could have listened to the soothing timbre of his voice long after it sank below the tree line. When the dining chairs grew uncomfortable, they migrated to the sofa and Daric called on a fire to stave off the morning chill.

Alaine could not remember a time when she had felt so at ease with another person. Even her relationship with her father had grown strained in recent years as he turned away countless suitors at her behest.

It was possible she knew more about Daric in a few hours than she did about anyone back home. Though none of it was anything she would deem important, it helped complete her picture of him and eased the concerns she had about living with him. She didn't know why his hatred of hats, fondness of roses, or appreciation for small, hand-carved wooden figurines made him less of a threat. All she knew was the butterflies that had plagued her stomach all night had finally calmed.

"And what of the outside world? I'm sure it has changed considerably in the years that I've been gone. What can you tell me about it?"

Daric's earnest curiosity was hard to refuse, though she noted the hint of sadness that flattened out the edges of his smile. "I'm not sure where to begin. To be completely honest, I don't know much about the outside world despite living there for all of my eighteen years." She chewed her lip, considering. A thought struck her and she smiled, holding her lip hostage between her teeth. "You'd probably hate it. Everyone wears hats now."

He chuckled and she almost purred in satisfaction at bringing the smile back to his face. He looked so much less beastly with a grin.

"It's true. The men all wear hats and the women bonnets, like one day hair became something vulgar to behold. And everything's a contest. Who can have the most gold? The biggest house? The prettiest wife?" She shrugged. "You'd probably find that not much has changed since you left."

"I very much doubt that."

The silence stretched between them and though it wasn't strained, Alaine felt their conversation coming to a close and rushed to fill the void.

"Tell me one more thing, Daric." It felt odd to call him by his given name, but she'd learned no other name or title. "What does one do with infinite time?"

In an instant, his eyes turned distant, the light within them shuttering behind a mask of cool indifference. She hadn't meant for it to be a deeply personal question, but she could see his turmoil as he debated how much of himself to reveal.

"I am probably not the best person to ask."

She opened her mouth to tell him he didn't need to answer, but he waved her off, taking a deep, bracing breath.

"In the early years, I did everything I could to escape. When that failed, I lost myself to rage. I burned the trees and uprooted every flower. I tore this cottage down, stone by stone. I tried to destroy everything, even myself." His words hung heavy in the air between them, but she had no comfort to give. His rage may have burned hotter, but hers was just beginning to spark. "After years—decades—I started to find myself again. I'd eat. I'd bathe. I'd chop wood and tend the garden, and at the end of the day, I'd sleep. What do I do with infinite time?" He shrugged. "I survive."

A shadow fell across them as a cloud passed before the sun.

Just a couple of years shy of seeing two decades herself, Alaine couldn't begin to fathom what it meant to endure centuries cursed as Daric has been. Would it be the same for her? How long until her mind became twisted by anger, her heart hardened by sadness? How long until she lost all hope?

She shuddered, suddenly cold despite the healthy fire burning in the hearth.

"Do not let my story dull your light." He smiled, but it didn't reach his eyes. "Would you tell me how you enjoy passing your time?"

"Well, it's nothing quite as exciting as *surviving*." She lowered her voice in impersonation of him, a weak attempt to lighten the mood, and his smile grew in appreciation of the effort. "I spend most of my free time reading."

He leaned back as though knocked off balance by her admission. "Is that a typical pastime for young women now? To read for pleasure? Can most people read and write?"

Of course literacy among women wouldn't have been as prevalent three hundred years ago. Alaine hesitated, unwilling to subject herself to the judgment and humiliation that was sure to come just as she'd begun to let her guard down. "I am fortunate to have learned to read and write, though I cannot say the same for most of the women in my village. My love of reading is generally not regarded favorably among the townspeople." She toyed with the sleeve of her dress, avoiding eye contact.

"I can't imagine why. I never took a liking to it myself, but if it brings you joy, there's no reason you shouldn't read."

His words eased a knot that had been forming in her chest. She had loved reading all her life. It was as much a part of her as her name. She'd hate to give it up now that she had seemingly endless time in which to do it.

"Have you tried asking the cottage for recommendations?"

She blinked, taken aback at someone encouraging her love of reading. It hadn't been a point of contention in her house, but neither was it supported. "It hadn't even occurred to me." Alaine turned like she was addressing a person, but realized that the cottage was all around her. It didn't matter which way she faced. She lifted her chin and spoke clearly. "I would very much appreciate some reading material, if you please."

Daric chuckled. "You're quite a bit more polite to our cage than I am."

"Yes," she said. "I suppose that is why you continue to receive burnt toast."

She looked around, expecting a small stack of books to appear on a table or shelf. When nothing occurred for several moments, Alaine shrugged, assuming the task to be too difficult for an inanimate structure. She ducked her head, embarrassed by the hope that had kindled at the thought of new reading material when a shift in the air caused the hair on her arms to stand. A tingling sensation at the back of her neck had her turning in her seat to find the space between their bed chamber doors expanding. She gasped as the wall stretched and pulled, a third door growing between the two.

Instinctively, she looked toward Daric. His expression was openly curious, not wary as she was after seeing such an incredible display of magic.

"After you, my lady." Daric sketched a bow and gestured grandly toward the new door.

Alaine held her breath as she crossed the room. There was nothing particularly ominous about the door itself, but she had only just adjusted to instant breakfast, she wasn't prepared for the cottage to sprout new rooms.

The doorknob warmed under her touch, like a reassurance from the house itself. She expelled a long breath, turned the knob, and pushed.

If she'd had any more air in her lungs, the room beyond would have knocked it out of her. She staggered back a step, reaching for the door jam. Daric was there in an instant, offering a supportive hand beneath her elbow and removing it as she found her footing. She smiled up at him, then turned back to the wonder before her.

It was not a large room, but ample sunlight filtered in through four tall, mullioned windows, making it feel grand and inviting. Two tufted armchairs beckoned from the center of the room, a small round table between them, and a plush rug beneath it all. She stepped reverently into the room and twirled in a slow circle, taking in the floor-to-ceiling bookshelves that lined every available wall. There must have been hundreds—no, thousands—of books, by her estimate.

She'd seen private libraries at various nobles' estates, but she'd always been an outsider, an observer. This was for *her*.

She trailed her fingers over the spines as she perused the titles. The familiar scent of leather and paper eased her last remaining worries. She took comfort in books in a way that she never could with other people. These were her friends, her confidants. They were entertainment, yes, but also an adventure, an escape—much like her current predicament. She didn't let her mind linger on the odd similarities.

"Thank you," she whispered, unsure if she was thanking the cottage, the witch, or Daric.

Selecting a book at random, she seated herself in one of the cozy armchairs and lost herself to another world.

CHAPTER 10

Daric

Daric found himself smiling more today than he had in hundreds of years. He smiled now as he thought of Alaine. When he'd left her, she'd been curled up in their newly acquired library, nose already buried in some book. Somehow, with her there, the cottage felt less like a prison. She had tilted his world on its axis and he couldn't tell if he'd been thrown off balance, or righted. Though he had spent centuries alone, her presence didn't feel invasive. She didn't demand attention, or really anything, for that matter. He admired her independence and stoicism. Skies knew he had not possessed the same poise and calm when he had first been cursed.

He doubted he was lucky enough for her to be the one to break his curse, especially with the witch's involvement in bringing her here, but suddenly being cursed didn't seem so bad.

The sun was still high in the sky when he strode outside. He plucked his axe from where it lay discarded from the day before. *Had it only been a day?* How quickly this woman had gotten under his skin. A day was a mere drop in the well of his life, but the ripples of this one shocked his still waters in a way he'd never felt before.

He hefted the axe and let it fall, splitting a log with a familiar crack. As with everything at the cottage, the woodpile could replenish itself without his aid, but Daric was grateful for the physical activity that kept his hands busy and his mind blank. His body quickly fell into the old routine, his thoughts free to wander. Only this time, they kept returning to Alaine.

After conversing with her for hours, it was clear that she was a woman that he could hold in high regard. She was so damn charming with her subtle humor and open honesty. He couldn't understand how someone so pure of heart could fail to see her worth beyond her supposed beauty. He'd bet anything that the villagers from her town had filled her head with this nonsense. He'd like to slaughter every one of them, though Alaine would likely protest such violence, even against those who wronged her.

He'd have to do better than that, be better than that—for her—for it was clear she deserved no part of this curse, no matter what the witch thought. He'd see her freed, even if it meant his return to solitude.

The ring on his finger glinted in the sunlight; his one reminder of the life he'd had—the life he'd lost. That life was gone to him, but he would make sure that Alaine never suffered the same pain.

By the time Daric split his last log, he'd devised a plan. He turned to go back inside and thought he caught a glimpse of fiery red hair darting behind a tree. The witch always seemed to be near—watching, waiting. Perhaps this was all a game to her, a source of entertainment. He knew not.

"It was a mistake bringing her here," he said into the wind.

The answering rustle of leaves sounded suspiciously like laughter.

CHAPTER 11

Alaine

A laine emerged from the library several hours later, eyes aching and stomach rumbling. She had finished an entire book before realizing it was the silver light of the moon shining through the windows and not the sun.

It had been only a day since she'd left her life behind, and yet it hung on the fringes of her mind like a distant memory. She had expected a mourning period of some sort. She thought she'd be crippled by regret or anger, but she felt only relief and—in the absence of the grief—guilt.

For the first time ever, Alaine lived as she wanted. Her actions were decided without a thought for other people. She missed her father, but in the way that one misses snow in summer, wistfully and fleetingly, her repressed anger overshadowing any happy memories from her life before.

She and Daric supped in companionable silence, each lost to their own thoughts. When the last of their plates had vanished in the magic of the cottage, they moved to what was quickly becoming their special place before the fire.

Alaine felt herself falling into a routine, but she wasn't upset by it. She tucked her feet beneath her, angling her body toward

Daric as he folded his massive frame onto the opposite end of the sofa.

"This has felt more like a holiday than a curse." She didn't mean for the words to slip out, but they had been echoing through her mind since breakfast. If she was honest with herself, being there felt like a weight had been lifted off her shoulders. It was easy to forget her responsibilities. Easy to forget the life she left behind. Easy to be there with Daric in their own little corner of the world. Like every part of her life leading up to this point had been a nightmare and now she was waking to find it all fading into the mists of memory.

She caught Daric's pained expression and instantly regretted her carelessness. "I don't mean to belittle your suffering. I can't even imagine what the past three hundred years have been like for you. I only meant that..." she hesitated, wondering how much to share. "I am enjoying my time here more than expected."

It was hardly a shameful confession, but the tips of her ears heated regardless. She struggled to meet Daric's intense gaze and found herself focusing on his lips instead—lips currently set into a grim line. She braced herself for his response, certain she'd offended him.

Seconds felt like hours as anxiety dug its claws into her mind. For better or worse, they were stuck together for the foreseeable future, and she couldn't shake the feeling that she had intruded on something precious. The possibility that she had ruined his life left a bad taste in her mouth, especially as she was feeling her life had just begun.

Daric's throat bobbed as he swallowed. When he finally spoke, his voice was gruff with emotion. "What I've been through is not your concern. I am here because of my own actions, but you—" He shook his head with a sardonic laugh. "You came into my life like a pebble in my shoe. After so long in stasis, the sudden change chafed. You were an unexpected distraction and I wanted to hate you for it."

Alaine deflated, her breath escaping in a heavy exhale. Her disappointment must have shown on her face because he rushed to continue. "I *wanted* to hate you, but I can't. You're...intriguing."

She lifted her brows, finally meeting his eyes with a look that conveyed her full skepticism of that assessment. Not that she wasn't flattered by the description; she just wasn't sure it could be true after she'd spent half the day alone in the library.

"What?" He chuckled and the warmth of it melted some of her petulance. "You're intelligent, funny, kind. You're exactly the kind of prison mate I didn't know I needed."

Alaine chuckled in spite of herself and considered his words. No one had ever described her as anything but pretty. *Intelligent. Funny. Kind.* She turned them over in her mind. Was that who she was? It seemed like a good start toward defining herself. They were labels she would be proud to wear, not that she had been ashamed to be beautiful. She'd only been shamed by the *reactions* to her beauty, the way it had been weaponized against her, but she refused to let these newfound traits be taken from her.

The small smile that lingered on her lips disappeared when she looked at Daric, who squirmed in the wake of his confession. She suspected it had been some time since he'd had any kind of meaningful conversation. That thought brought back the sobering reality of their situation. As much as she enjoyed their time together, they were still cursed. *Daric* was still cursed, and that didn't sit well with her.

"Well, if today was any indication, I think that witch made a huge mistake when she cursed me. A housemate who's a great conversationalist and a magical cottage that provides unlimited reading material? Some curse." She smiled, but Daric didn't return it, his expression serious.

"I must admit, this curse is much more enjoyable with your company, but I sincerely regret that you've been dragged into my personal Hell. However, I think if we both combine our efforts, we could get you freed in no time."

Alaine blinked at him, providing him ample time to take the words back or tell her it was a joke, but he remained silent, watching as she absorbed the full weight of what he'd said. "I just told you I'm happy here and you're ready to send me away?" she snapped. She couldn't help it. A lifetime of searching for a place where she could be herself and here he was trying to free her, to get her to leave. "I've no interest in being freed."

"You've only been here a day. You have no idea what it's like waiting day in and day out for nothing—"

She jumped to her feet. "And you have no idea what it's like out there. To be a *female* out there! To be primped and prodded and leered at and bargained for." She knew her anger was misplaced, that he only wanted to help her, but she couldn't help the years of frustration that suddenly overwhelmed her.

Alaine's blood was boiling now, the heat of the fire becoming too much in the small space. As though sensing her burning rage, the fire in the hearth winked out, plunging them into darkness. Her breath was coming too fast compared to Daric's deep, steady breaths. His unaffected state only made her angrier.

How could he be so calm about this?

"What about your family, Alaine?" Even his voice was calm and yet she shook with rage. "What about your father? You'll just leave him behind?" The guilt she'd been suppressing resurfaced at his words, but she refused to be cowed.

"I would gladly live out the rest of my days here."

Finally, she hit a mark and Daric exploded to his feet. She felt the air he displaced as he shot up, felt the anger rippling off him in waves to match her own. The shadowed outline of his massive form unnerved her, but she didn't shrink in the perceived safety of the dark.

"And what if there is no end?" he roared. "What if thousands of years from now, we're still the same two people rising with the same sun, while everyone you loved, everything you knew, was nothing but dust in the wind? What if you regret the chance you missed to see your father again? What if the loss and longing drive you mad? And there's no cure for it because there's no end to this curse."

Was she mistaken or had his voice taken on a haunted edge as though these were his own fears being spoken aloud? He quieted, seeming to reign himself in and when he spoke again his voice was softer, but no less sharp. "What if you realize that the lives you live between those pages are nothing compared to living it for yourself? What then, Alaine? I can't sit here and watch you throw away everything I've desired for the last three hundred years. I won't."

His tone brooked no argument, which was just as well because as far as she was concerned, the conversation was over.

"Light, please."

A single taper appeared on the small dining table, providing just enough light to ensure she didn't stumble on her way to her room. She made sure to extinguish it before slamming her door, leaving Daric in complete darkness.

CHAPTER 12

Daric

That could have gone better, Daric thought as the ghost of the light finally faded from his vision.

Plunged into the familiar dark, he sighed, wondering how he could convince Alaine to see reason. He understood better than most the pressures of being desired for one aspect of a person. The expectations to look a certain way, act a certain way, live a certain way. But accepting the curse was not a solution. Sure, being secluded to a cottage in the forest seemed better with company, but it was only a matter of time before she tired of him and desired her freedom. He was saving her the trouble of wasting all that time in between. It had nothing to do with his fear of getting attached to her. Nothing at all.

He sighed again, sprawling out on the tiny sofa. His head landed where Alaine had been only minutes before, the sweet scent of lavender and honey lingering in her absence. He'd been doomed before, but now he was doubly doomed. That witch knew exactly what she was doing by sending Alaine to him.

He'd grown complacent, resigned to his situation, and had no hope that he would ever be free. Alaine might be trapped here, but her curse was his to bear. He knew he would feel the sting of her loss more acutely than the endless loneliness.

Though he disagreed with her choice to stay, he admired her for standing up to him. Not many had the courage to do that in his former life. He'd spoken true when he called her intelligent, funny, and kind, but that was just scraping the surface of who he already knew her to be. He'd known her for no time at all, but she'd proven herself to be quietly confident, optimistic, headstrong, empathetic, and thoughtful. The more he knew of her, the more he liked her—and that was territory his heart wasn't prepared to enter.

Still, if he'd learned anything from his enchantment, it was never to take anything for granted.

He sat up slowly and rolled his shoulders in an attempt to shake off the weight of his decision. He could do this. Alaine could stay for as long as she liked. He would do nothing to assist her freedom if she didn't desire it. Her company would be a welcome reprieve and he would enjoy every second spent with her. When she finally tired of him or found a way to be free from the curse... Daric shuddered. He would deal with that when the time came. He'd dug himself out of despair before. He'd just have to take this day by day.

With one slow exhale, his shoulders sagged. He could do this. He *would* do this. For Alaine.

"One day at a time, Daric."

CHAPTER 13

Alaine

A laine woke the next day with swollen, aching eyes, blinking against the brightness of her sunlit room. After she'd stormed away, her anger had turned to frustration until the unexpected release of tears had left her hollow. Daric had opened an old wound, the familiar sting doing nothing to help her sour mood.

All she wanted was a place to belong; to be worthy of existing in a space without expectation.

She extracted herself from under a yellow blanket dotted with pink embroidered roses that mocked her dark disposition. Balling it in her fists, she threw it on the floor, though she knew the cottage would replace it on her bed as soon as she left.

The wood floor felt cool beneath her feet as she slipped from the bed. She regretted having left her shoes behind when she entered the forest and frowned down at the same blue dress she'd been wearing for two days. A bath would be nice, but she'd settle for a clean dress and new shoes.

A tall, ornately carved armoire beckoned her from across the room. Alaine made it all of two steps toward it when a pair of fur-lined slippers landed on the floor before her. A squeak erupted from her mouth before she could stifle it and she rolled her eyes at her knee-jerk reaction. She might never become accustomed to the magic of the cottage.

The slippers were soft and warm. A low groan escaped her lips as she slipped them on her feet. Walking the rest of the distance felt like dancing on clouds compared to the last couple days. She opened the armoire and frowned at the selection of pastel and jewel tone dresses. There was everything from linen and lace, to velvet and satin, but none of it appealed to her somber mood. She slammed the doors closed, tipping her head forward to rest against the cool wood.

With her gaze cast downward, her vision snagged on her slippered feet. She wanted to kick herself for forgetting—yet again—that she was in an enchanted cottage. An enchanted cottage with no obligatory social etiquette.

"Cottage, would you fetch me something different to wear? How about something darker? Maybe a little out of the ordinary? And no stays, if you please," she added as an afterthought. She'd had enough of propriety. If Daric could walk around half naked, he could allow her this one comfort.

The tingling sensation that she'd come to associate with magic swept over her face. She fought against the urge to sneeze as she stepped away from the armoire. With cautious excitement, she eased the doors open, revealing a brand new wardrobe of dark garments.

She fanned through a dozen dresses from modest to scandalous, and even several pairs of trousers and shirts, her fingers hesitating over them before deciding on a simple blousy frock and a quilted bodice, both in ebony.

Her body slipped easily into the loose dress and she made quick work of the front lacing on the bodice. The sleeves were intended to be cinched at the wrist as well, but she left them loose, fisting the material and hiding her thumbs within. The scalloped hem hid her shoes well enough that she decided to keep the slippers on. She'd already spent most of her time here barefoot anyway. She knew Daric wouldn't judge her.

There was only a small, polished silver on the table in which to view herself, but she didn't much care how she looked. With a twirl, she marveled at the freedom the garment afforded. Feeling emboldened by her color choice and the lack of restraint, she hoisted up the skirt and danced around the small room, humming as she pranced and turned without a care for the problems that awaited outside her door. She leapt onto the bed and bounced with abandon like she had as a child, embracing the feeling she thought lost forever.

When her legs ached and her chest burned, she collapsed in a fit of giggles, burying her face in a pillow to suppress the sound.

She panted as her laughter subsided. Pulling her face from the pillow to gulp down air, she choked as she saw her surroundings. Coughing and sputtering, she sat up and took in the room anew.

Gone were the pale pinks and sunny yellows, the white washed wood and bouquets of wildflowers. Instead the room was bathed in warm, earthy hues that echoed those of the forest beyond the window. Dark wood furniture glowed in the golden light of the sun. Every spare inch of space was dripping with dark pink and burgundy roses. A wrought iron chandelier hung over a richly woven rug of mossy green. Her fingers dug into the plush, velvet bed covers, the deep teal perfectly matching the color she imagined the ocean to be.

She smiled at the transformation, wishing she'd had the presence of mind to bring a book to bed with her the night before.

"Thank you for redecorating," she addressed the cottage. "Do you think you could bring me a book?"

Alaine waited, but when none appeared she figured it was either ignoring her request or unable to grant it. Whatever the reason, she still couldn't bring herself to leave the room.

She dreaded facing Daric after their heated conversation and opted instead to break her fast in her room. The cottage obliged this request, providing her a small stack of crêpes and simple tea service on the desk by the window. Taking a seat, she frowned at the sight before her. She needn't have worried about running into Daric in the cottage because she had a clear view of him toiling away in the garden from her window.

He sat at the base of a tree, leaning against the trunk, his head bowed in concentration over whatever he held in his hands.

Fixing a cup of tea, she took the opportunity to watch him unnoticed, appreciating his muscled form yet again. She couldn't deny his attractiveness, but she couldn't admire him outright without becoming self-conscious of her own appearance. She knew she was being just as bad as all the villagers in her hometown, believing herself unworthy of his attention because she no longer possessed comparable beauty. His desire to help free her had felt too similar to the rejection she'd been expecting since she'd first glimpsed her new face in the mirror. He had called her homely, after all. Perhaps remaining cursed was setting her up for heartbreak, but she couldn't bear the thought of returning to her provincial life yet. Yes, she needed to discover who she really was so she could define her worth on her own terms and not through the eyes of others. But maybe she could make a friend along the way, provided said friend could remove the stick from his derrière and accept her choice to stay.

She fumed at the reminder of their spat, hoping things could return to the way they'd been before he'd suggested she leave. She had quickly come around to the idea of spending the rest of her life here. She just needed *him* to feel the same way. Otherwise, she was no better than an intruder.

In the time it took to finish her meal, Daric's focus never wavered from the object in his hands. Curiosity piqued, Alaine figured she'd indulged in self-pity long enough and decided to join him in the garden.

From the cover of the cottage, she'd failed to notice the foreboding cast of clouds that hovered overhead. The wind had picked up as well, bringing with it a chill that whispered of the coming frost. Thinking of winter brought to mind her parents back home and the debt that hung over their heads. She didn't know what they would do without her there to marry Baxter, but at the moment she was still too vexed to care. They had at least a month before the first snowfall, even longer until the debt was due. That should be plenty of time to come up with the money needed, or to find evidence of Baxter's lies.

She shook her head to clear the unwanted thoughts. If her family could sell her off to Baxter so easily, she couldn't be blamed for seeking a different path in life. She hadn't made the choice to be here, but she was making the choice to stay, though her family's fate weighed on her conscience still.

She shivered as she picked her way through the high grass to Daric, pausing when she caught sight of the wicked blade in his hands. She couldn't see what he was doing with it, only the surety with which he handled it.

Butterflies awoke in her belly and with them came the memory of rough hands on tender flesh. There was always that undercurrent of fear, of knowing he could hurt her if he chose.

He had yet to show any sign of aggression, even when they'd argued, but she'd seen firsthand the speed at which a man's temperament could change.

"Alaine."

The sound of her name had her blinking away darker thoughts. Daric was staring at her expectantly and she suspected he'd been trying to coax her from her brooding for some time.

"Sorry." She shrugged. "It seems my mind was elsewhere."

Daric pursed his lips but didn't remark further. For a moment, their gazes held. No words passed between them, but she could read those left unsaid in his eyes. He wouldn't apologize, and neither would she, but it was behind them. They had too many tomorrows ahead of them to fret about yesterday.

Alaine nodded tentatively toward the object in his hands. "What are you working on?" It was an olive branch, a peace offering. She was willing to move on if he was.

Daric held the object aloft and she approached warily. Their hands met as he deposited it into her palm. A small thrill ran through her at the contact, distracting her from the nerves that plagued her. He pulled back first, glancing away as though self-conscious.

"It's a gift," he said as she turned it over in her hands.

She couldn't believe what she beheld. The rose was like nothing she'd ever seen. Intricately carved from wood, the delicate details made it look as though it had been plucked from the bush itself.

"You made this?" she asked incredulously.

He tipped his chin down and she could have sworn she saw the hint of a blush before he ran his hand over his face. "I know that when you mess up, you're supposed to give a girl flowers, but you seem like the kind of person who'd appreciate something handmade. So, I did both."

"It's fitting, I suppose, to receive an immortal rose from an immortal man."

He winced at the mention of his immortality. "Do you like it?"

Alaine couldn't help the smile that spread across her face. "I love it," she said.

Daric's answering smile crinkled the edges of his eyes. He stood up and clasped her free hand in both of his. "I want you to stay."

The sincerity in his voice almost brought her to tears, but she fought the emotion swelling in her chest and responded truthfully. "That's good, because I want to stay."

CHAPTER 14

Daric

Alaine stared at him like he'd given her a puppy. He could tell she was on the verge of tears as she cradled the wooden rose in her hand. He hoped they were happy tears after he'd botched his attempt at an apology. He'd spent all morning rehearsing what he would say, only to have the words fly from his mind the moment he set eyes on her in that black dress.

It wasn't even the dress so much as the way she wore it. Her shoulders were back and her head held high, though her chin dipped just slightly in a manner that dared anyone to question her. She was magnificent. In that moment, he saw a queen, and the prince in him damned every obstacle that stood in the way of making her his.

He still struggled with her decision to stay, but at the end of the day, it was *her* decision and he would not try to voice his thoughts on the topic again. Looking at her now, she seemed happy enough with her choice that it eased some of his gnawing doubts.

The sky chose that moment to open up, unleashing the pouring rain that had been threatening all morning. Alaine squealed as the first cool drops hit her skin and sprinted for the door. He followed close behind, his long strides quickly making up the distance between them so he was there to catch her as she slipped. It was the second time they had touched that day and both times had sent a shock through him, like the spark between them was trying to restart his heart.

With the excuse of the rain-slicked ground, he kept hold of her as she found her footing, taking her hand and guiding her through the deluge.

Her fingers looked delicate next to his, but she gripped his hand with a ferocity that belied her softness. When they reached the cover of the thatched overhang, he finally relinquished his hold, immediately missing the gentle warmth of her skin.

Alaine slipped inside the cottage as he held the door open. He shook himself off, dispelling as much water as he could before joining her. She stood just inside the door, toweling herself off. He wondered if she'd asked for the towels or if the cottage had simply anticipated their need. The magic was curious like that. She handed him a second towel as he entered, but it hung limply from his hand as he openly gaped at Alaine's appearance.

The witch may have taken her beauty, but the black dress, now plastered to her body like a second skin, accentuated her feminine curves, the low neckline highlighting the pale skin of her décolletage. Her hair hung loose, the damp locks springing naturally into gentle waves. Though her eyes were swollen, likely from the crying that had eaten at him all night, a light glimmered from within, the first hint of hope he'd seen from her since he'd told her she should leave.

She gave him a questioning look when she caught him staring, but he waved her off. Towel in hand, he attempted to dry off, giving up after the task proved futile.

"Why don't we both change into something dry," he said. "Then, I'll meet you at the fireplace with some hot tea."

"Good idea. See you in a moment." Alaine rushed to her room, a trail of water in her wake.

Daric peeled off his shirt and wrung it out in the kitchen sink, placing it over the back of one of the dining chairs as he swiped up the towel to finish drying off. He was almost to his bedroom door when Alaine's cracked open. It would have been the fastest he'd ever known a woman to change, but he glanced over and saw her peeking out at him between the door and the frame.

"Is everything alright?" he asked, concern lacing his voice.

She glanced down and fumbled with the ties of her bodice. If he didn't know better, he'd say she was embarrassed. He thought he heard her mutter something under her breath, but the words were lost to her cleavage.

"I'm sorry. What did you say?"

She tilted her head up, looking him square in the eyes. "I said I can't seem to undo this knot with it being all wet." Her eyes dared him to laugh at her, but he failed to see the humor in the situation. If anything, she'd just helped his body temperature rise.

He looked down at the laces entwined in her fingers. "Right. Well, I don't know how much help I can be, but I'll give it a try." A knot of his own formed in his throat and he swallowed against the tightening sensation as he stepped toward her.

Her hands dropped to her sides and she glanced away as he brought his face closer to her chest, attempting to ignore the way the rain magnified her sweet scent. His fingers were clumsy as they ran over the knot. They were much too large and his nails too short to pick apart the dainty knot. Pulling on the ends proved pointless as well.

"How attached are you to this bodice?" he asked casually.

"It's just a bodice," she said. "I'm not attached to it in any way other than physically."

"Good."

Before she could move away, he leaned forward and grasped the ties in his teeth, tearing them apart with a quick yank.

Alaine yelped in surprise as she hurried to hold together both sides of the bodice, though her dress beneath covered everything—much to Daric's dismay.

Her cheeks were flushed as he stepped away. "Thank you," she said breathlessly and retreated into the confines of her room.

"You're quite welcome," he said as she closed her door. While he meant for the words to be polite, the deep growl of his voice betrayed his wicked thoughts. He quietly berated himself all the way to his door, utilizing the colorful language he'd had centuries to hone. He'd kick himself if he made things uncomfortable between them, but maybe it was for the best. Obviously he couldn't be trusted to keep his hands to himself. Alaine would need to be the voice of reason for them both.

CHAPTER 15

Alaine

Alaine pressed her back to the door, chest heaving from the brief interaction with Daric that left her panting. She'd never been intimate with a man, had never even considered the notion until Daric's mouth had been a mere breath away from her breasts.

She'd been kissed before, of course. Though she'd never kissed anyone.

That was the distinction.

The action had always been initiated by the other person. She was always the kissee and never the kisser. As such, it had never seemed quite as magical as her books made it out to be.

Though Daric had freed her from her bodice with quick, efficient movements, her body still reeled from the agonizing closeness of him. For the first time in her life, she was overwhelmed by the utterly foreign urge to kiss someone. It could not have been a more inconvenient time to be struck by a crush.

Alaine closed her eyes and inhaled the soft scent of wood smoke and rain. She waited until she heard the quiet *click* of Daric's door closing before she finished undressing. Her clothes were soaked and getting them off was far more difficult than she'd anticipated. She briefly considered asking Daric for his help again, but she forced her thoughts away from the improper desire, chastising herself for the way her skin heated at the memory of him tearing through her ties with his teeth.

He was a *beast*, but he was still a man, and she would be wise not to tempt him. Still, she wondered how it would feel to have his rough and calloused hands running over her body, his captivating mouth nipping at her skin.

She shivered and goosebumps sprang up on her arms, reminding her that she was still half soaked and completely naked.

"Something dry, if you please, cottage," she said, her voice muffled by the towel as she dried her hair. "Doesn't have to be black."

She looked out from under the towel and saw a stunning, red dress laid out on the bed. While the material looked appealing, the neckline looked rather low.

"Something a bit more casual, I think. There's also no reason to remind him I'm female if you know what I mean," she whispered conspiratorially.

A puff of wind blew her damp locks back as the cottage seemed to sigh in annoyance, but the dress disappeared, a simple tunic and pants replacing it. That wasn't exactly what she'd had in mind, but she supposed it would do. He certainly wouldn't think she was seducing him. Or maybe he would... Men were funny like that.

She put the breeches on first, fumbling with the gusset ties in the back, but refusing to ask for Daric's aid again, particularly because she was topless. Once she'd gotten the pants to stay up, the tunic was easy to slip over her head. It was smaller than she expected but still shapeless. Her curves were less pronounced, her cleavage completely hidden.

Satisfied, she grabbed a blanket off the bed, throwing it over her shoulders to hide the majority of her ensemble. Daric's brief touch had already chased away most of her chill, but her stomach churned at the thought of stepping out in men's clothing.

Daric was seated before the hearth, steaming cup in hand as she stepped out her door. The now familiar crackle of burning wood was drowned out by the howling wind as the rain continued to fall, battering the windows. If the cottage wasn't enchanted, she would be concerned for its structural integrity. As it was, there appeared to be no drafts or leaks to speak of—only the cozy, warm glow of the fire.

If Daric noticed her outfit, he didn't mention it as she sat down beside him, picking up her own cup of tea from the table. It was a marvel that the cottage always prepared it exactly to her liking. She inhaled the sweet, floral scent and warmth seeped into her fingers.

"I never used to light the fire before you came."

She jumped at Daric's sudden confession, taking a moment to turn over his words in her head before she could process them. "But you always chop firewood..." she said, her voice trailing off in question.

He nodded slowly, staring at the fire. "It was something to do, but the firewood—" He gestured to the pile before the hearth. "It replenishes itself without my help. I just couldn't stand it, the warmth and the light. In my home, we always ate dinner as a family before a giant hearth." Though his mouth twitched upward, his eyes glinted with repressed memories. "The fire reminds me of all I've lost. I didn't feel worthy of basking in its glow. Rather, I embraced the cold and the dark; they were my punishments for the choices I made to get me here."

"Are you certain it was your choices that got you here?" She asked, suddenly curious.

"It was an impossible choice, but it was mine to make."

The bleakness in his tone sent a shiver down her spine. Thunder rumbled as she curled farther into the blanket, seeking shelter from the chilling conversation.

"I'm sorry. I didn't mean to sound so melancholy. I wanted you to know that you've brought light to my life in more ways than one. I told you that I want you to stay and I meant it. Losing you would be like losing the sun, for though I cannot look directly at its beauty, I can see it in the way it makes the flowers bloom. I fear I am blooming for you, Alaine, and I will selfishly yearn for your light for the rest of my life."

Words stuck in her throat. She had no response to such a proclamation. He spoke as if her departure was inevitable, despite their shared desire for her to remain.

She set her teacup on the table and slid her hand over his, feeling him tense beneath her touch. "I'm here now," she whispered, the words feeling inadequate next to his.

"I'm glad," he said, taking her hand in his.

His thumb stroking her palm made her shiver for an entirely different reason.

CHAPTER 16

Daric

D aric woke to the gentle weight of Alaine pressed
against him, her head nestled against his arm like
a pillow. They hadn't moved from the sofa. Though he'd
sensed her beginning to nod off, he'd been unwilling to
surrender her hand to rouse her. It wasn't long before he
too had given in to the sweet embrace of sleep. For the first
time that he could remember, sleep had come easy and been
undisturbed by terrors and restlessness.

He blamed Alaine.

Surely, her presence acted as a calming balm to his soul
even in slumber. While he wanted to attribute his improved
mood wholly to her, he couldn't be sure that it wasn't simply
the lack of loneliness. But Daric had always been lonely,
even before being cursed, even constantly surrounded by
courtiers and servants. That was his problem all along. He
had known early on in his life he was incomplete. A vital
piece of himself was missing, the sharp edges of which grated on him constantly.

The sofa creaked as he let his head fall back. He held his
breath as Alaine stirred, only exhaling once her breathing
resumed the deep, even rhythm of sleep.

His fingers tingled and he tried to wiggle them without shifting too much. Still unwilling to extricate himself, he glanced at her from the corner of his eye, squinting at the sunlight streaming down from a window he would swear had not existed the previous day.

One glance around confirmed all the windows were open, a cool breeze wafting in from the east. The storm had passed, leaving behind the clean, earthy scent of petrichor; the smell of new beginnings and fresh starts.

He hated how much Alaine felt like the start of something new. Hated that he'd already become attached to her presence, her voice, her touch, her laugh. If he dug himself any deeper, he could end up buried alive.

As much as he enjoyed her company, he couldn't accept her staying with him indefinitely. And he would not let himself fall for her, for surely falling in love would only lead to a broken heart. Although he was beginning to think that breaking may be preferable to the surviving he'd done before she arrived, the guilt of his acquiescence ate at him. He couldn't shake the feeling they'd both made a terrible mistake, but he wouldn't force her hand. The choice was hers to make.

Knowing he would rather lie with her all day, Daric forced himself to get up, gently positioning Alaine flat on the sofa so she wouldn't wake. He froze with his hand hovering over her, barely resisting the urge to sweep her hair out of her face. Only half a handbreadth lay between them, and try as he might, he couldn't shake the desire to close the distance and touch her.

He yanked his hand away, confused at the emotions rolling through him. Yes, he cared for Alaine. How could he not when she'd proven time and again to be kind-hearted and understanding? He feared he'd spent too much time away from others to recognize if it was blossoming into something more, or just a desperate desire to form an attachment. Any attachment.

He couldn't trust that any of this was genuine and not due to the witches meddling after all, but one glimpse at Alaine had all his doubts turning to smoke.

The scent of her clung to him, driving him mad as he went about preparing breakfast. There wasn't much to prepare since the cottage did most of the work for him, but he asked for dishes she seemed to prefer, and a vase of roses.

"Forget the roses," he whispered to the cottage. They weren't courting after all.

The roses were slow to disappear, as though the magic disagreed with his choice. He supposed no excuse was needed to do something nice. He scrubbed a hand down his face as he reconsidered. "What do you think?" He'd never spoken to the cottage as something with a consciousness, never expected a response, let alone an opinion, other than the completion of a task, but when the roses rematerialized, he considered them thoughtfully. "Good choice."

"Are you talking to yourself?"

He jumped, looking over his shoulder to see Alaine fully awake and watching him from the sofa, a coy smile playing on her lips.

"I was speaking to our cage." No sooner had he responded then the entire house began to tremble. The windows rattled, the furniture rocked, and the roses spilled onto the floor, the vase shattering into tiny pieces.

Daric sprang into action, rushing to shield Alaine from any falling debris. The quake stopped just as suddenly as it had begun. In a whir of movement, the furniture righted itself. The vase and flowers became whole once more and sat serenely at the center of the table. Daric stood from his place over Alaine, his mouth agape, unsure what to do for fear of it happening again.

"I don't think the cottage likes it when you call it a cage," Alaine whispered out of the side of her mouth.

In answer, Daric's plate crashed onto the floor. Alaine's answering laugh was instant, bubbling out of her like steam from a boiling pot. For once, she tried to capture it in her hand, attempting to spare him the humility no doubt, but the sight of her doubled over, shaking and wheezing into her hand, had a barking laugh bursting from him before he could think to contain it. This sent her into a proper fit. She flopped back on the sofa and promptly slipped off the edge, landing on the floor with an ungraceful *thud*.

As tears began streaming down her cheeks, Daric rushed to check on her, thinking she'd managed to hurt herself. She waved him away as her laughter subsided and brushed the tears away with the back of her hand. His cheeks hurt, but he couldn't fight the upward tilt of his mouth as he helped her to her feet. Placing her hand in the crook of his elbow, he led her to where their breakfast awaited.

"The roses are a nice touch," she said, sending him a conspiratorial grin over her shoulder as he pushed in her chair.

He winked as he took the chair opposite her, feeling the start of something new and hopeful take root in his chest.

They spent the rest of the day together. Alaine talked with him as he chopped wood and he sat with her while she read. They didn't speak of curses or regrets, but sometimes their eyes would meet and she'd burst out laughing, and every single time, Daric felt the world shift beneath his feet. Change was coming and he held no hope that it would be good, but he vowed to cherish the time they had together, however brief it may be.

That night, they settled again on the sofa before the fire and spoke into the dead of night. It was no surprise when Alaine drifted to sleep and Daric fought the urge to sleep beside her again. He considered waking her, or carrying her to her own bed, but decided it was best not to disturb her.

"Blanket," he whispered and the cottage obliged, leaving a small quilt folded beside her rather than over her as he'd intended.

Now the damned house was playing matchmaker?

With more force than intended, he snatched up the blanket and gently draped it over Alaine's still slumbering form.

"Well, this is cozy."

The words echoed in his ears like the memory of a nightmare. It was the voice of the one that had cursed him, and the effect it had on him was instant. He froze, a chill racing down his spine and wrapping around his innards. He'd never learned her name, only called her what she was: the witch. In a flash, fear became anger, thawing his frozen limbs.

Daric whipped around, piercing his enemy with a stare that expressed all he wished to do to her. She'd never dared to appear inside the cottage, always waited for him at the fringes of the forest.

This time she appeared as the maiden, exactly as Alaine had described, exactly as she'd been the first night she'd come to him. Her long red hair swayed in a breeze he couldn't feel and a cruel smile slashed across her face. Every time since he'd been cursed, she appeared to him as the crone; a hunched, wicked looking creature that haunted his nightmares. Skies help him, it took everything in him to contain the rage he felt at seeing her in this form yet again.

"What do you want, Witch?" he growled the words as much as spat them out. "Haven't you done enough meddling in recent days?"

"I've just come to check how your new arrangement is faring." Her voice was dripped in honey; a fake sweetness sure to poison the ears of anyone who heard it.

"Is that what you call this?" He gestured to Alaine, lowering his voice as he remembered her sleeping state. "An arrangement?"

"I grow weary of you, Prince Daric." She inspected a blackened fingernail, feigning boredom when he knew he was her favorite form of entertainment. "You've just been so... dull. I thought I might liven this place up a bit. Have a bit of fun, if you will."

Daric clenched his fists, annoyed at being reduced to the witch's personal jester. "And? Are you thoroughly entertained?"

"Well I might be if you two would actually *do* anything." She threw her hands up in exasperation and disappeared in a cloud of smoke.

Before Daric could breathe a sigh of relief at her departure, he sensed her at his back. He whirled reaching for the blade sheathed at his side, but her focus was on the still sleeping Alaine.

"She really is a pretty thing, Prince. I wish you could see."

Her hand reached out as though to caress Alaine's cheek and he lunged without a thought, catching the witch by her wrist and throwing her back.

"Don't touch her," he snarled.

The witch threw her head back and laughed, a great cackle that shook the dust from the rafters. It was then that Daric noticed no *crackle* or *pop* sounded from the burning logs in the fireplace. He needn't have worried about waking Alaine since whatever the witch was doing seemed to be containing all sound.

"I knew leaving her beauty untouched would make this too easy, but I had no idea you'd fall for her so fast without it," she said as she clapped her hands together in giddy amusement.

"What are you talking about, you mad woman?" He resisted the urge to rub out the headache that was forming behind his eyes. He needed to keep her in his sights at all times and strike if ever there was an opportunity.

"You're falling in love with her."

He staggered back as though physically struck. "She's been here three days. You wouldn't know love if it stabbed a blade through your blackened heart." His own blade lifted in emphasis.

She looked at him sidelong with one raised eyebrow and his arguments died on his tongue. He'd already admitted to himself that he cared about Alaine. He felt responsible for her curse. Not only that, but she was a good person and a joy to be around. Anyone would feel the same way about her. She was infectious and addictive, but he would know if he was falling in love with her. Unless he was deliberately ignoring his feelings in an effort to save himself from heartbreak. Though, that was putting a lot of faith in his subconscious. He shook his head to dislodge the thought, like he could forget the four letter word by sheer force of will.

"What is it that upsets you, Daric? Perhaps Alaine is exactly what you need to see yourself freed once and for all."

"I'm not holding my breath."

The witch shrugged, her lips twisting to one side as though she could care less, but Daric knew he had her full attention now. She'd come here for entertainment. Well, he could be entertaining. He felt a renewed sense of hope as a dangerous idea took shape.

His face must have revealed his thoughts because the witch squinted at him in curiosity.

"What are you thinking, Prince?"

He licked his lips, suddenly nervous. "I'd like to propose a bargain."

"You're in no position to bargain." She crossed her arms, regarding him with renewed interest.

"I'd like to bargain for Alaine's freedom."

Her pupils dilated and he knew he'd piqued her interest.

"Go on."

"Alaine must fall in love with me, right? That is the way to break my curse." The witch neither accepted nor denied his claim, but Daric pushed on. "Give her one year, one year from the day she was cursed, to fall in love with me. If she doesn't love me after a year, you'll let her go."

"And why would I agree to that?"

"If you free her of your own accord, I'll give you what you always wanted." He took a deep, steadying breath. "My crown."

The witch huffed out a laugh. "You know nothing of what I want. Besides, your kingdom is long gone, torn apart by wars and lost to the ages. You are a prince of nothing."

Daric had long suspected it, but hearing her confirm the truth of it was like a punch to the gut. Still, he was desperate to see Alaine freed.

"Me, then. You can have me."

She froze and Daric could see the thoughts whirring behind her eyes. She wanted him. He knew not in what capacity, sensed he would regret offering this bargain if he ever found out, but he had her in his grasp, ready to do as he asked.

"I already have you."

"Do you really, though? I'd be yours to do with as you will. No more curses, no enchanted cottage. Just me." He considered dropping to his knees, would have if he thought it would grant him any favors.

"You would give your life for hers?"

"Yes," he answered without hesitation. With that one word, Daric confirmed what they both already knew. What he'd been fighting for days. He loved Alaine. He might not be *in love* with her. Yet. But somewhere along the way, his feelings of affection had burgeoned into something far deeper.

"Interesting." She drew out the word, her expression inscrutable as she raked her eyes over him. "Very well. I accept. You have three hundred and sixty-two days left, Prince Daric. Enjoy!"

Her echoing laugh lingered long after she faded from view, but Daric knew she was gone when a log popped, startling both him and Alaine. She sat up suddenly, blinking away sleep as she took in her surroundings. When her eyes found his in the dim light, he gasped.

The witch was right. She was beautiful.

CHAPTER 17

Alaine

A laine sat up, instantly alert. "What is it? Has something happened?" She cast around for any hint of danger but she saw no one other than Daric, knife drawn as he stood above her. Old habits had her flinching away before she could remember herself, remember who was with her. She trusted Daric enough to know he wouldn't hurt her. She didn't know how that trust had been built in so short a time, but she didn't question it.

Daric's eyes darted away from her and he rubbed a hand down the back of his neck. "The witch was just here."

"What?" she screeched, jumping to her feet. "Why didn't you wake me? What did she want?" Her emotions were bouncing from shock to anger to relief that he was okay. That last one brought her back to shock, unsure when had she begun to care about his well-being.

"I think she had you spelled. She cut off all the sound in the room."

She sensed there was more he wasn't telling her as he shifted from side to side. His eyes continued to look anywhere but at her and a growing sense of dread took root in her gut.

"Well?" She waved her arms, drawing his attention back. His eyes searched her face and immediately flicked away. Reflexively, she brought her hand to her face, probing fingers searching for any new flaws the witch may have inflicted. When her search came up empty, she reached out to Daric, taking his hand in hers and squeezing firmly. "Talk to me. What did she want?"

He shook his head mutely and her frustration rose. She gripped his hand tighter, causing him to wince. "What did she do, Daric?" Her voice rose in pitch with her panic and he seemed to finally realize what keeping her in the dark was doing to her.

"She only came to play. We're her entertainment." He spat the last word like it left a foul taste in his mouth. "Nothing happened. Well..." He winced again, but this time it wasn't from her grip. His eyes met hers, finally holding her imploring gaze. "Almost nothing happened."

"What is that supposed to mean?" Rather than alleviate her fears, his cryptic answers only magnified them. She released his hand, stepping away to catch her breath. It was so hard to breathe around Daric, but she didn't have the time to analyze that reaction either. This night was full of unexpected revelations.

She rubbed damp palms down the front of her skirt, catching sight of her frenzied face in the looking glass above the mantel, and stopped cold.

Her face.

Her face.

She gasped, mimicking the sound Daric had made when she'd awoken. Tentatively, she traced the contours of her face, wondering how she failed to notice the difference when she'd felt it earlier. She whirled and found Daric watching her with barely veiled concern.

"You can see me. The real me, I mean. My real face."

He only nodded, seeming at a loss for words.

She wasn't sure how she felt about him seeing her. It had been a relief of sorts to hide behind the face that wasn't her own. She'd felt no attachment to it and thus harbored no resentment at its criticism. But with it gone came all her old fears, the expectation that she owed the world her beauty and it owed her nothing in return; the subsequent need to prove she was more than her outward appearance, that the sum of her parts included her mind, her heart, and her soul.

Alaine turned to face Daric fully, lifting her chin to meet his eyes as defiance blazed from her own. "And?" she asked. "What do you see?"

It took Daric a moment to answer and she worried she'd pushed him past his comfort. They might have shared an intimate few days together, but before those days, they were strangers.

His focus shifted from her eyes and she felt the brush of his gaze as it roamed her features. It didn't burn as Baxter's had. Rather, it was a caress, light as a feather, gently stroking her face.

His eyes returned to hers and she saw no hint of the possessiveness she often found in the eyes of men. In fact, he looked at her as he always had, without judgment or pity. It warmed her to see no change in him.

"I see the same young woman who accepted a terrible fate with grace, who lit up with the discovery of a library, whose kindness and stubbornness brought a smile to a face I wasn't sure capable of the feat." He stepped closer, invading her space, but she welcomed the closeness, inhaling his scent of pine and wood smoke. "You *are* beautiful. It is impossible not to see it. But your face is only a reflection of the woman I know within."

Alaine glowed from the inside out. She'd been complimented before, but this was different. Daric *saw* her, beyond the pretty picture her features painted. Her cheeks hurt from the joy that pulled up the corners of her mouth, but it was worth it to see the same smile mirrored on Daric's face. As one, they fell into each other, wrapping themselves in a comforting embrace that felt as natural as falling asleep.

Is this what it feels like to fall in love? Alaine thought, immediately striking the thought from her mind. People didn't fall in love after only knowing each other for three days. Stepping away, her smile transformed into something shy and tentative as Daric's hands lingered at her elbows.

"I should probably go to bed," she said.

"Right. Sure." His voice was more gravelly than usual and he cleared his throat as his hands fell to his sides.

Her instincts roared at her to step back into his arms, already missing their warmth and steadiness. She fought the desire, for the sake of her hopeless heart, if nothing else.

Her feet pointed in her intended direction, but she couldn't make them move. It was almost like she wanted to live in this night forever, not that she needed to add another aspect to this curse.

Finally breaking free of her indecision, she forced her feet to move, one in front of the other. She paused beside Daric and rose on her tip-toes to place a feather-soft kiss on his cheek.

"Thank you," she whispered.

His eyebrows drew together. "For what?" he asked, his voice soft like hers, but lower. A growl that awakened butterflies in her stomach.

"For seeing me."

That night Alaine dreamed of possibilities she'd never allowed herself to consider.

CHAPTER 18

The Witch

The Ancient One clenched Their fists as the scene unfolded in the witch's scrying mirror. Jagged nails punctured the skin of Their palms, but They couldn't be bothered to care. The witch had almost ruined everything.

They felt her then, she whose body They inhabited.

Eudora.

Something had roused her from the dream-like state in which They kept her, nestled within her own subconscious. Something that invigorated her spirit. Made her fight back. She didn't understand that They were protecting her, protecting all of them from the full power of the curse.

She must have stored her magic these years, hoarding it while They'd had to waste precious energy sustaining her fragile body. It had been a mistake to wear the maiden's form during Their visit. The crone took far less effort to maintain.

Twice tonight she'd broken through Their defenses. The first time, she accepted that foolish bargain with the Prince. It changed nothing in the end. If anything, it might entice him to work harder for their shared goal.

They were that much closer to being free of this mess, but then Eudora had gone and returned the girl her beauty. It had happened suddenly as They were departing, Their magic so depleted They didn't notice the subtle spell until They'd spied the girl in the mirror moments ago.

That risk could have spoiled all Their hard work in a matter of minutes. Of course, he would fall in love with the girl. Even after hundreds of years, he was still desperate for love. The girl, however, was not so easily convinced—even less so now that he could see her true face. Her beauty sowed seeds of doubt, and doubt was a weed not easily eliminated.

That damage could set Them back years, and it was time that They didn't have to spare. Already, Their magic weakened. The additional work of containing the girl stretched Them close to the limits of Their mighty gift.

They screeched in frustration, casting the mirror away. They couldn't even spare the effort it would take to travel back to the cottage and assert some damage control over the situation. They would need to wait until Their magic replenished. Likely by morning.

That meant They had all night to consider Their next move.

It was no matter, though. They refused to be beaten at Their own games.

The spark of an idea ignited. Their lips split, revealing broken and yellowed teeth. Though They needed to fan the flames, They knew without a doubt that the battle was not lost. In the morning, They would visit Alaine.

CHAPTER 19

Daric

Daric managed to stay upright until the door to Alaine's room closed. With the *snick* of the latch, he collapsed into the waiting arms of his chair. The events of the night had wrought havoc on his nerves. At once, he felt hollow and full to bursting. He had so many emotions battling for control within him: fear, relief, hope. Things he hadn't felt in years. And yet, there remained an emptiness too. A sense of foreboding that might only have been his self-sabotaging anxiety rearing its ugly head. But he knew better than to blame instinct on anxious thoughts.

He wanted to tell Alaine of his new bargain with the witch, but apprehension kept him from rising to knock on her door. She'd be furious to learn that he planned to have her freed in less than a year. While he hoped she would one day break his curse, he wouldn't use this information to influence her feelings toward him in any way. Perhaps if she grew tired of the curse, if she grew weary of the monotony, then he would tell her *something*, but not a moment sooner.

One year.

Less than one year, if he was counting the days. It was hardly any time at all in the grand scheme of things, and then he would be free of this prison. He had to admit he'd been thinking of it as a cage less and less since Alaine had joined him there. For better or worse, he would soon be leaving. The question was, would he leave with Alaine or the witch?

Chapter 20

Alaine

Morning dawned swift and unwelcome, frost coating the window panes after a rapid drop in temperature overnight.

Alaine approached her looking glass with trepidation. Worried she had dreamed the whole thing, and yet also hoping she had. She couldn't decide how to feel about having her face returned to her. For years, her beauty had been a curse in itself. While she had mourned the loss of the face she knew, it had been a welcome respite from the expectations and judgment that came with being beautiful.

As her reflection appeared on the silvered surface, she forced out the breath she'd been holding, still unsure if it was disappointment or relief that caused her shoulders to drop. Her face glowed in the soft sunlight, the same face she'd known most of her life, still as pretty and perfect as it had been the night before.

She sighed again and slumped into the seat in front of her.

She was being ridiculous. There were far more important things to worry about than the restoration of her beauty, like the unsettling appearance of the witch, or the looming debt that she'd inadvertently saddled on her family, or the words spoken between her and Daric last night.

Of the three, the last was the least concerning, but it was the one that sat at the forefront of her mind, refusing to be pushed aside until she'd examined it from all angles.

Was he falling for her? Was she *falling for* him?

The idea both confused and excited her. She'd never imagined there could be room for love in her life. A marriage to a man she tolerated, who found her tolerable in return—that was all she had dared to hope for.

Daric was far more than tolerable. He'd been kind and funny and, most importantly, he *saw* her. She never felt more herself than when she was with him. It was the oddest feeling of completion, as though they were two halves of a whole, split apart by time and distance, only to be brought together by mere coincidence. Or was it?

Her lips tipped up at the corners as she thought about a life with him, a simple life in the forest with her days spent immersed in books and her nights before the fire with Daric.

"Would you like me to change it back?"

Alaine jolted as she spotted the withered, old hag in her looking glass. She whirled, searching every shadow and crevasse, but there was no sign of the witch in her room. However, when she turned back to the mirror, the hag remained.

"How—how are you doing this?" Alaine forced the words past her shock.

"Wouldn't you like to know?" The witch bared her broken, yellow teeth. "I can take your beauty away again, if you'd like. I'm sure it must be such a burden."

"Since when do you care what I'd like? If you're so interested in helping me, set me free." She was through playing games for this witch's entertainment. "I'm not even sure why you gave me back my beauty. It does nothing to further your end."

"And what would you know of my end?" A wicked gleam entered the witch's eye and Alaine held her tongue, knowing that speaking would create more questions than answers.

The witch clicked her tongue. "You do amuse me, dearie, but have you considered Daric's opinion of your beauty?"

The question startled Alaine. Of course she hadn't considered his opinion, no opinion mattered but her own. She told the witch as much and frowned at the resultant cackle.

"He's falling for you, yes? Has he told you that much? Surely, you have seen the evidence of it with your own eyes?"

Alaine whipped her head to the door, hoping Daric wasn't near enough to overhear their conversation. Though she'd already begun to suspect as much, her cheeks burned at the witch's frank words.

Apparently, her body language was answer enough for the witch.

"And did you notice this happening before or after I returned your face?"

"That's not—" Alaine began, but the witch clicked her tongue again.

"I didn't ask if *you* had feelings for him before, but if *he* had feelings for you."

The days blurred together and Alaine suddenly found herself unable to distinguish when his feelings had become apparent. It couldn't have only been the night before. Surely, she had seen some inkling of his affection before then. Unless she had been the one to initiate each of those moments. Perhaps she was reading into his actions too much. He hadn't kissed her, hadn't professed any feelings for her beyond liking her. That was hardly a declaration of love.

He'd been kind to her and while that put him far above any other man she'd known, it didn't mean he loved her. He was a good man—but also a lonely man. And he hadn't loved her. At least, not until he'd seen her face.

"Men are all the same," the witch crooned. "He might claim to love your soul, but love isn't blind. What was it he called you when I first delivered you?"

"Homely," Alaine whispered. That word had been the one source of doubt that picked at her resolve. It echoed in her mind like the taunts of school children.

"Ah, yes! Homely." The witch clapped her hands gleefully, at odds with her ancient exterior. "As Prince Daric mentioned, he has certain standards to uphold. He might have appreciated your character when you were plain, but he didn't really consider you worthy of love until he saw the *real* you."

The room plunged into semi-darkness as the sun retreated behind the clouds. Alaine clutched the table to keep from swaying as the reality sunk in. She'd been foolish. Daric was charming, but he was just another man blinded by beauty. His words were nothing more than empty platitudes. As she pondered this, her mind registered the rest of what the witch said.

"Did you say Daric is a prince?"

"Oops. Did I say that?" The witch looked anything but apologetic as she shrugged. "Oh well. I suppose you would have found out eventually. How very convenient that he holds a position powerful enough to see your family freed from its debts."

The walls closed in and the air became thin as the crushing weight of guilt slammed down on Alaine. It had been so easy to forget that life went on outside these walls, that back in her village her parents were scrambling to meet a deadline that was fast approaching without the assurance of marrying her off to Baxter. She hadn't even considered how they must feel about the disappearance of their only child. Her father would be beside himself.

"So, what will it be, Alaine?" Her name sounded foul on the witch's tongue. "Shall I leave you to your beauty or take it away?"

Alaine was torn. She had no use for her beauty—certainly no fondness for it—but it remained a part of who she was and she didn't like the idea of having to transform her body to live the life she wanted. If ever she found herself freed from this, it would be a burden, but one she would only have to bear until it fades, as beauty always does.

She needed to be freed. She needed to save her family, and if that meant marrying Henrik Baxter, then she would need her pretty face too.

She took a steadying breath, squared her shoulders, and gave the witch her answer.

CHAPTER 21

Daric

It was nearly midday and Alaine had not left her room. Daric understood that the events of the night had been traumatic, he'd barely slept himself, but he was beginning to worry that something was truly wrong.

He convinced his feet to make the journey to her door and was working up the courage to knock when it swung open untouched. Alaine jumped back, startled to see him on the other side of her door. Her beauty took his breath away, as it had the night before, and he silently berated himself for letting it affect him so. She was still the same person he'd come to admire and he vowed to treat her no differently for her lovely face.

"I was just coming to check on you," he said, his voice rough.

She nodded, but wouldn't meet his eyes. His first instinct was to reach for her, but her hunched shoulders and crossed arms discouraged his touch. He stepped away, giving her space to enter the living quarters. She shuffled past him a shell of the woman she'd been just hours before. He thought they'd had a moment last night before she'd retired. He was sure they had both felt the fire building between them, but this morning he felt only chills. He didn't know what had changed.

She sat at the table and he hesitated before taking his usual seat across from her. In the clear morning light, he saw a rift opening between them. Whatever they'd shared during the evening hours by the fire, it had slipped through his fingers as night turned to day.

The table between them may as well have been a wall. He didn't know how to bridge the distance that seemed determined to separate them. His hand itched to reach out, craving a physical connection as the silence stretched on. He hadn't had the stomach to eat when he'd first awoken and now, looking at Alaine, he wondered if she would also have no appetite.

"Would you like something to eat?" he asked.

"Why didn't you tell me you're a prince?" Her voice was sharp and cutting, nothing like the Alaine he'd come to know.

"I—what? I wanted to, but I couldn't." A half lie. He couldn't have told her thanks to the curse, but he liked her not knowing. It was a part of himself he had no control over. It was a birthright, a curse in and of itself, with its own set of responsibilities and prejudices. He liked that she could know him without the crown looming over his head. In that way, he supposed it was much like her beauty. "I guess we're even now."

"Are you keeping score?"

Her voice cut at him, reminding him of the cruel court ladies. "No, I just meant that you can see all of me as I see you."

Her expression softened at that and she turned contemplative.

"Would you have told me, even if you had been allowed?"

Shame colored his cheeks, but he didn't want to lie. "Not right away."

She nodded, but her face held no judgment.

"What I am is not the same as who I am, but once people learn that I am royalty, it colors their opinion of me from that point forward. I wouldn't have kept it from you if you'd asked, but neither would I have told you unprompted. It was a new experience for me and I didn't want to tint the lens through which you viewed me."

A rueful smile twisted her lips. "Will you tell me about it now?"

"I can try." He poked around for the magical gag that usually coalesced when he tried to speak about his past. Nothing. His breath escaped in a long exhale as he pushed down his trepidation. He opened his mouth expecting to choke on his words but found that they flowed as though he had never been cursed. "I *was* a prince. I suppose I still am, though I no longer have a kingdom to speak of. I was the heir apparent. From the time I could walk, I'd been groomed to take the throne. Told how to stand, what to say, when to eat. There was nothing that was my own. The courtiers demanded I marry, as though sharing my bed with a woman would make me a better king."

He caught a hint of rose tingeing Alaine's cheeks before she turned her face away and he hurried on to save her embarrassment. "The court ladies...they were not what I wished for in a bride. Don't get me wrong, they had their assets, but they only ever sought my crown. They cared not for the man beneath it."

Alaine remained silent but her eyes warmed, revealing some of the kindness he'd come to expect from her.

"The witch came to me as the red-haired maiden, just as you'd first met her. I had no idea she was an enchantress. She posed as a woman of the court, traveling from distant lands to visit family. I thought she sought to win my heart, speaking of true love and fairytales, and maybe she did. I never knew her true intention for visiting. I sent her away like the rest of the court girls, not knowing at the time that she possessed such magic. Three days later she returned, but she was different."

"Different how?"

Even the memory of her appearance had his heart rate increasing. Her crazed visage haunted his nightmares to this day. "She looked like she hadn't slept in all the days she'd been gone. Her hair was a knotted mess. There were dark circles beneath her eyes. Even her cheeks had hollowed like she hadn't bothered to eat. But the muttering. Constant, incoherent ramblings. She'd become something out of a nightmare. In my hubris, I thought she'd gone mad from my rejection." He shook his head ruefully, his embarrassment coming back to him in full force. "I was so mulish then. I didn't take her seriously."

"You sent her away," Alaine finished for him.

"I tried to. The guards must have underestimated her. She broke free from their grasp and the second she touched me, I was transported here." He dropped his head in his hands and when he spoke again, his voice was muffled. "I've considered my decision every day for over three hundred years, but I'm not sure there ever was a choice. If I wasn't trapped in a cottage, I'd be trapped in a marriage. I was cursed from the first moment I sent her away. From that action forward, my life was not my own."

Daric sighed, feeling like a great burden had been lifted from his shoulders. He lifted his head to meet Alaine's gaze, contemplative where he expected to see pity.

"What are you thinking?" He knew it wasn't his place to pry, but he constantly wanted to know what was going on behind those deep brown eyes.

"It might be nothing, but," Alaine bit her lip, considering. "If my face was restored and you can speak about your past, maybe the curse is broken?"

The hope in her voice nearly broke him.

"I thought you liked it here," he joked, trying to lighten the mood. He wouldn't admit how much it hurt him to think of her leaving.

"I did. I mean, I do," she backtracked. "It's just with the witch showing up, I've come to realize how much we are just pawns in her game. I guess it takes the fun out of it."

The right side of her mouth turned up in a semblance of a smile, but Daric recognized the effort behind it and matched it with one of his own. He sensed she was only telling him part of the truth, but he let the matter fall. This was as good a time as any to tell her of his latest bargain with the witch. Maybe her mood would improve if she knew her sentence was only temporary.

"Alaine, I want you to know that I—" Daric choked, neck spasming as he tried to dislodge the words that stuck in his throat.

Alaine jumped to her feet, a look of concern creasing her brow as he coughed violently. Rushing to his side, she thumped him on the back until the fit subsided into great heaving gasps. He wiped the tears from his eyes and gratefully accepted a glass of water that Alaine proffered, nodding his thanks before taking several large gulps.

By the time he regained most of his composure, Alaine had resumed her seat, concern still pulling at the corners of her eyes. He ran his fingers through his hair and groaned when he realized what had happened. "It would seem the rules of the game have changed." Of course, he wouldn't be able to tell her.

By changing the parameters of their agreement, he'd altered what could be considered pertinent information.

He stewed in silence as he considered what this new information meant for them, but something niggled at the back of his mind, something off.

He studied Alaine anew. Something had changed in the hours since he'd seen her last. When they'd bid farewell, she had been disturbed, but amicable, nothing like the cold and distant woman who had emerged from her room today.

"How is it that you came to know of my title?" he asked as casually as he could muster.

Alaine kept her eyes downcast as she answered. "The witch visited me this morning."

"What?" Daric exploded out of his chair, clenching and unclenching his fists. He knew he should have stayed with her last night. His desire to maintain decorum had kept him from imposing, but the idea of the witch coming to her when she was alone in her room had him seeing red.

"It wasn't exactly a visit, per se," Alaine clarified. "She appeared to me in my looking glass."

Daric's feet moved of their own volition as he stalked from one corner of the room to the other, the distance too short to take the edge off his anger. He was a caged beast and he wanted blood. "Did she say why she came to you?"

"Not in so many words," she hedged.

"Alaine!" His frustration was a palpable thing, like a small child repeatedly poking at a sore spot. "What did she want?"

In response, Alaine thrust her jaw forward, glaring at him with the force of a thousand suns. If he hadn't been so afraid for her at that moment, he would have stopped to admire the expression. No other could make him contemplate his life choices with one look alone.

He rushed toward her, reaching to touch her, to assure himself of her safety. It was the first time he'd reached for her in urgency since that first day. He'd almost forgotten her reaction then, but this time, he froze no more than a handbreadth from her, rendered completely immobile by shock as she flinched from him.

CHAPTER 22

Alaine

"**W**ho hurt you?" Daric's voice was lethally calm as she opened her eyes to find him frozen mere inches away.

"What are you talking about? No one hurt me." She couldn't understand why he was having this reaction. "The witch just talked to me. She wasn't even really there in the room. I think it was—"

"No," he interrupted her rantings. "In your past, at home, in your town, wherever it happened, someone has hurt you. This—" he gestured to her tense, fetal-like position, "is not normal."

She forced her limbs to relax, placing her hands in her lap and willing her trembling legs to still. How could she tell Daric about Baxter? Daric was everything Baxter was not, but Baxter existed in the real world. In her short life, she'd known more men to be like Baxter than Daric. "It's—"

"Don't you dare tell me it's nothing." Though his voice still held a hint of the anger simmering beneath the surface, his brows creased in concern.

Alaine had to wonder if it stemmed from a place of curiosity, or if the witch was wrong and he did care for her.

She saw no harm in telling him about Baxter. Though it shamed her to think of what he and others had done to her, she hoped it would help to have someone else share this burden. She fixed her gaze on the table, unwilling to see Daric's reaction as she told her tale. If he looked at her with any amount of pity, she might just curl up on the floor and die of embarrassment.

"There is a man in my town, Lord Baxter. He desired me in a way that became borderline obsessive. He sought my hand in marriage, but I refused on numerous occasions. His advances grew more... forceful with each refusal."

Daric remained silent. She could feel the anger rippling off him like steam, but he didn't interrupt her.

"The day that I arrived here, I'd had another run-in with Baxter. He was rougher than usual. I think his patience was finally wearing thin." She blew out a breath, blinking back tears. "My first instinct is to brush it off as nothing, to make excuses for him. That's just the way things are. Men can't be expected to control their temper. It was *my* fault for leading him on and then refusing him. I'm so tired of it. I'm tired of fighting, tired of defending myself, tired of a world that sees me as less than worthy because I'm a woman."

She laughed bitterly. "Before I ended up here, I'd finally decided that I was going to accept his proposal. My family—" she swallowed against the knot that formed at the memory, "Baxter agreed to clear a rather large outstanding debt in exchange for my hand. It is their last resort." Her cheeks heated in the wake of her admission and she drew her finger along the table grain to avoid meeting Daric's probing gaze.

Strong fingers enveloped hers in a reassuring grip. His thumb stroked the back of her hand as a strangled sob escaped her.

"If I ever see that man, I will personally repay all of his wrong-doings tenfold. I swear it on my honor."

She finally looked up at him, seeing no judgment or pity, only grim resolve to uphold his promise. The overwhelming urge to kiss him shocked her so thoroughly, she forgot her misery. She wondered if he'd be gentle, if the contrast of his soft lips and rough stubble would drive her wild, but she sobered at the recollection of the witch's words. He hadn't kissed her before she was beautiful and, though he maintained a respectful distance aside from his hand stroking hers, she couldn't be sure that any interest from him now wasn't purely due to her appearance.

Sliding her fingers from his, she tucked them in her lap as he reclaimed the seat across from her.

"What a pair we are, eh?"

She appreciated his attempt at levity, answering his rhetorical question with a half-smirk of her own. It didn't reach her eyes, but neither did it reach his.

Things had certainly changed between them. All the hope she had felt rising these past couple days had burned to ash in the wake of the witch's machinations.

"Is there nothing we can do?" She didn't need to elaborate. He knew she was talking about the witch and her endless schemes.

"You don't need to worry. I—" He cut off with another strangled sound and Alaine knew there was more he wished to tell her, but couldn't.

However he'd been about to finish that sentence, he was wrong. She had plenty to worry about, not the least of which was her traitor heart falling for the man before her, a prince whose love she could not trust.

She should have accepted the witch's offer to change it back, but she didn't trust her either. There had been no cause for the witch to restore her beauty to begin with and if she wanted to take it back, that was a good enough reason for Alaine to keep it.

Frustrations mounting, she pushed back her chair and retreated to the one place she knew she'd find peace and solitude: the library.

CHAPTER 23

Alaine

Alaine tossed and turned in her plush ocean of blankets. She'd avoided Daric for the rest of the day, taking her supper in the library and retiring to her room as exhaustion weighed down her eyelids. She'd wanted the time to dissect his words, but she was no closer to figuring out the truth of his heart—or her own, for that matter.

Lying awake in her darkened room, even the soft sounds of the forest could not comfort her. Her heart was heavy. In discovering she was cursed, she thought all her problems had been solved. She thought she'd escaped her marriage to Baxter guilt-free, and found a place where she could be herself. Instead of relief, however, a nagging sense of shame ate away at her. She'd abandoned her family without a thought, too quickly accepting the perfect illusion of her cursed fate and refusing Daric's offer to help free her.

Now, she felt stuck.

Though Daric had guessed at ways to free her, she didn't know how to accomplish what was needed of her. If she was honest, a small part of her still wished to remain. Her mind and her heart pulled her in different directions and there was no telling which side would win—or if she'd be torn apart before a victor could be declared.

Giving up on sleep, Alaine swung her legs over the side of the bed, grateful for the soft rug beneath her feet as she plodded across the room. She paused at her door, listening for any signs that Daric was awake on the other side. When only silence greeted her, she cautiously turned the knob. Through luck or magic, the door made no sound as it swung inward.

Though only embers remained in the fireplace, a soft, golden glow lit her way through the dark. She stoked the fire until its warmth staved off the worst of her chill. She thought to ask the cottage for a cup of chamomile tea and lose herself in another book until sleep claimed her, but she found herself stopping outside Daric's door rather than the one that led to the library.

She didn't know what had brought her here. He likely slept on the other side. Even if he was awake, she had nothing more to say to him.

Still her body refused to move on. Her hand raised of its own volition, poised to knock before the carved wood. She wondered if Daric had been the one to carve the images into its face, or if it was merely another trick of the cottage. In all her days at the cottage, she hadn't paid any mind to what was carved on her own door, but she relaxed her fist to trace the details in Daric's. A light sweep of her fingers revealed an intricate landscape with towering mountains and sweeping forests. When they brushed over the parapets of a grand castle situated between the two, the door swung inward and she nearly toppled over into the darkened room beyond.

Alaine stumbled back, fear igniting in her chest, though she'd done nothing wrong by admiring the door. She clutched her chest, waiting for an imposing silhouette to fill the doorframe, for the threats and shouts she knew better than to expect from Daric. None came.

Before she could think better of it, she rushed forward to close the door, pausing on the threshold as a strange sound reached her ears.

Daric's usually deep voice cried out from darkness. His frantic shouts set alarm bells pealing in her head.

Her first thought was that the witch had come to torture him in some new and terrible fashion.

She would not stand idly by while he was so obviously in distress. Shoving decorum aside, she hurled herself through the doorway.

A small beam of moonlight barely illuminated the space and it took longer than she would have liked for her eyes to adapt to the dim light. She moved as fast as she dared, keeping her arms outstretched as the intoxicating scent of him surrounded her, guiding her forward.

Daric's labored breaths called to her from the opposite end of the room.

She worried she was too late.

She worried the witch had come for him.

Hurt him.

Or worse.

She quickened her feet, pushing aside the nagging feeling that it could be a trap. If the witch had wanted her for any reason, she could have taken her whenever she pleased. But if she only wanted to cause her pain, then hurting Daric was the fastest way to get to her.

Her vision adjusted and she was stunned to find the room largely empty save for a grand, four-poster bed. The witch wasn't here—not that she could see. A large form shifted beneath the covers and the realization of what she was doing washed over her. She'd barged into his private chamber while he slept. There was no cause for alarm, no threat. She bit her lip wondering if she'd misjudged the situation.

Deciding to leave before she woke him, she backpedaled away from the enormous bed. A floorboard creaked beneath her foot and she froze as Daric whimpered, the sound so broken she wondered if he was hurt after all.

Then he began murmuring. Faintly at first, but steadily growing louder with each repetition of the same word over and over again. "No."

"No. No. No. No. NO. NO. *NO!*"

She was at his side in an instant, his words becoming one unending roar as he battled an invisible foe. His fists swung wildly and she dodged flailing limbs in a futile effort to sooth him. She switched tactics, shouting his name, but his cries drowned out her own.

At a loss, she could only watch helplessly as he raged, her own heart breaking at the fear in his voice, the pain etched into his features.

Eventually, his bellows turned to sobs and the fight left his limbs. She approached the bed with trepidation, concerned for her own safety as much as for Daric.

Curled on one side, he looked for all the world like some forlorn child. His hair was mussed and a deep line remained etched between his brows. She wiped away the tears staining his cheeks with soft, soothing strokes.

He roused at her touch. Eyes cracking open, he blinked up at her around swollen lids.

"Am I dreaming?" he whispered.

Alaine shook her head. "Not anymore."

He sat up suddenly, bringing his face dangerously close to hers. Rather than pull away as she usually would, she leaned in, drawn to the honest vulnerability in his expression. He seemed to take in her presence in his room with a mixture of disbelief and awe. In the charged space between them, it felt as though lightning could strike at any moment.

The silence stretched on as she gazed at him. She wished she could know the thoughts in his head, wished she could read them on his skin as clearly as she could the pages of a book. They had learned so much about each other in her time here and still she craved more. She wanted to know him as one only could after spending a lifetime together. The idea both thrilled and terrified her, but it was Daric's quick glance to her lips that had her finally pulling back.

As they separated, the tension in the room ebbed. Alaine exhaled a shaky breath and crossed her arms, tucking her trembling hands out of view.

This wasn't how she'd intended the evening to go.

"I wanted to see if you were alright," Alaine muttered. She glanced away, no longer able to hold his gaze in light of her admission. "You were crying out in your sleep," she finished sheepishly.

"Thank you," he replied. "Unfortunately, I find I am plagued by frequent nightmares. I'm sorry if I woke you."

She shook her head. "I couldn't sleep. I was just about to get some tea when I heard you. Would you care for some?"

"No, thank you."

Alaine wondered if his formality was meant as a polite dismissal or if it was merely a lingering habit from his days as a royal.

"Well, I'll let you get back to sleep," she said, turning to leave.

"Wait."

Alaine froze at the command in his tone, but she didn't move to face him.

"Stay." His voice broke on the word and he cleared his throat to try again. "Please stay. I could use a friend right now. If you want to stay, that is."

She knew she shouldn't, not when this tenuous thing growing between them threatened every intention she had of returning to her family, but the sincerity in his voice gave her pause. Whether or not they could be more, Daric *had* become her friend and she wouldn't deny him this comfort when it was hers to give.

"Move over, then. I shall tell you stories until you can sleep again."

He smiled and pushed himself back to the other side of the bed, leaving more than enough space for Alaine to join him. The ghost of his warmth was a welcome solace as she slid into the vacated space.

She rolled onto her side to face him like he was her and felt a jolt of panic at the intimate position. Never before had she laid in bed with a man. It was wholly improper and yet, some small part of her relished the indecency of it.

She cleared her throat, hoping her voice did not betray her nerves, and let her words fill the air around them. "Once upon a time, there was a little boy who could not lie."

And so she went, retelling stories from her youth until Daric's breaths turned to deep rumblings of sleep. All the while, she refused to bridge the gap that stretched between their bodies like a raging river dividing the land into east and west. It wasn't the physical act she avoided, rather the emotional connection she feared it would forge. Daric was something special and it would be all too easy to give up everything to make a life with him in this enchanted cottage.

Alaine slipped from his room in the early morning hours. As the sky began to brighten with the coming dawn, she bid farewell to the night and to the last hope she had for remaining with Daric. For it was a new day, and she was determined to be free of this curse.

CHAPTER 24

Daric

For weeks after his nightmare, Daric barely saw Alaine. She had been gone by the time he'd awoken and could scarcely seem to make eye contact with him after. Their meals—when they shared them—were quick and silent. More often, she spent her time in the library. They no longer spent the evenings together on the sofa before the hearth, no longer swapped stories until the early morning hours. He wanted to give her space, but he got the feeling she was avoiding him and he didn't know why. Though they still occupied the same cottage, still suffered the same curse, he missed her. If her presence had been a balm to his soul, her absence was like pouring salt in a wound. He carried the sting of it with him always. It never dulled, never eased.

He'd taken to chopping wood again, anything to fill the endless silence. There was no doubt in his mind that he'd messed up. Somewhere along the line, she had decided he was not worth her time and he couldn't help but feel the witch's visit had changed her opinion of him. Alaine still hadn't told him why the witch visited her the morning after she restored her beauty, but he knew he could fix it, if only she'd give him a chance. He just didn't know how to convince her that he was worthy of that chance.

His latest destruction lay in a heap around him. As he gathered the split logs, he racked his brain for any kind of solution that would see both him and Alaine free at the end of a year. Frankly, he should be grateful that the witch had accepted his bargain at all. Knowing Alaine would be free no matter what eased the tension in his neck, but he longed to taste that freedom side-by-side with her, perhaps even hand-in-hand, if she would have him. That thought seemed ridiculous given their current situation, but he refused to give up hope of a happy ending again. He wouldn't return to that pit of despair until all was truly lost.

The autumn sun was weak, the air crisp and cool, foretelling the coming of winter. Soaked in sweat, he shivered, feeling the bite of the wind now that he'd abandoned his task.

He glanced toward the cottage, the picturesque scene never failing to mock him. If this was really his home, and Alaine his wife, he'd be the happiest man alive. But it was nothing more than a prison disguised as a utopia. Alaine was not his. Though he considered himself fortunate that the curse had brought them together, it left him feeling guilty. The idea that he had ruined her life chased away any pleasant associations.

As though summoned by his thoughts, he caught a glimpse of Alaine through one of the windows, glowing in the muted sunlight. She was striking. Having gotten to know the person within first, he knew that her face matched the beauty of her soul. It was appalling that those she'd grown up with had failed to see her value as a whole. Beauty fades, but a good heart is forever. He'd much rather be with the latter than the former, though apparently, that made him the minority among men.

If only he'd figured all this out before everything changed between them.

Alaine moved out of view and he realized that she was in the library, a fact he should have known given the amount of time that she spent there recently. He was glad that the library provided her even a small bit of happiness. With all the reading she'd been doing, he wouldn't be surprised if she finished every book in there before their year was up.

A thread of an idea formed at that last thought. If he followed it, he just might repair his relationship with Alaine. With the cottage's help, he only needed to wait until she retired for the night.

He stacked the last of the firewood and set about making the preparations. Everything would need to be perfect, but if his plan worked, maybe he could win back the heart of the woman who had stolen his.

CHAPTER 25

Alaine

Alaine slid the book back into place on the shelf. None of her tried and true favorites were holding her interest. Months ago, her heart ached to read adventurous stories and tales of other lands. Now, it ached for another reason.

She let her fingers skim the spines as she walked beside the shelf, her subconscious mind wishing she was running her fingers over the hard planes of Daric's body. Yanking her hand away, she chastised herself. It was the romance novels invading her thoughts. She'd already ruled out the possibility of a future with Daric. Unable to trust his affection or even his friendship, she had all but ignored him these past several weeks, and it hurt. She missed him, but she wouldn't risk her hopeful heart. The loss of him, coupled with the knowledge that she may one day become Mrs. Henrik Baxter, nearly broke her. Still, she had decided to do right by her family.

There were potentially only a few weeks remaining until the first snow, less than that if she was unlucky. Daric had guessed that all she needed to do to be free was learn her true value. It couldn't be that hard. Then, she'd be free—free to marry Baxter and save her family—and Daric would remain, imprisoned within the cottage grounds. *That* would be the hard part.

If she was honest with herself, she felt worse about someday leaving him to his loneliness. She could no more sacrifice his heart than she could her own. Better that they remain unattached. That was what she told herself to get through the days, and it helped a little.

Not for the first time, she wondered how to break his curse. If she knew they could have something together beyond the curse, she'd be more inclined to follow her desires.

Perhaps she could puzzle out the mystery of Daric's curse. He'd been able to share so much about his past, but the details of his enchantment remained unknown to her. She knew they shared similar reservations when it came to forming attachments, unable to know a potential partner's true intentions. His royal title had been stripped from him as well. Could his curse be as simple as hers? It seemed unlikely that he didn't see his worth after three hundred years of solitude, but that didn't feel right anyway. Daric had known his worth beyond his title when he'd refused the witch initially.

She collapsed onto one of the plush armchairs, defeated and certain that her thoughts were going in circles.

"Cottage." She felt the shift in the air as the walls awaited her request. "How can I free him?"

A faint breeze ruffled her hair, though the windows were firmly shut. She got the sense the cottage had just sighed in response to her inquiry, but then she heard a heavy thunk and looked up to see a large, black tome on the table before her. The title gleamed in gold inlay and Alaine rolled her eyes when she read it.

"*A History of Love?*" she scoffed. "You don't have to mock me. I asked for help, not advice."

She bit back a yelp as a stack of books rained down to land on top of the first. *For Love or Death, True Love's Kiss, Young Love*, and on and on, each title containing something related to *love*. Plucking one off the top, she fanned through the pages, blowing out a breath as her eyes skimmed the text. Her thumb paused on a page and she read a few lines aloud.

"He looked at her like she was the world, like she was his sun and moon and stars and losing her would mean losing everything." Alaine's voice had taken on a wistful quality. It was too much to ask that someone could look at her that way. She'd stopped hoping for the fairytale, but now that she was living some kind of twisted version, she wondered if happily ever after was possible after all. Or was she doomed to live out a vicious cycle of heartache and expectations for the rest of her days?

She made to replace the book on the top of the pile, but thought better of it. Tucking it beneath her arm, she strode out the library door and right into the immovable bulk of Daric.

Daric's arm shot out to catch her before she could fall. She couldn't say the same for her book. As it tumbled to the floor, she recalled this same thing happening with Baxter and endeavored to take better care of watching where she was going.

Too soon, Daric's comforting touch was gone. He never allowed his hand to linger longer than was necessary and she regretted his decency at that moment. Though they bent to retrieve the book at the same time, Daric reached it first, snatching it and holding it up to the light. He squinted as he read the title.

"*Hopeless Love?*"

That was the title? Her cheeks flamed. Of all the books for the cottage to send her.

"Give that back!" She easily yanked the book from his proffered hand, trying and failing to ignore the smile he fought to hold back. She growled and threw him the meanest look she could muster. "The cottage recommended it."

"I'm sure it did." Amusement twinkled in his eyes.

Alaine turned her face away to hide the smile that spread across her lips. He was so infuriatingly charming, it made it hard to deny her budding feelings for him. She fisted her hands in her skirts and redoubled her efforts, walking over to the dining table and sitting in her usual place.

Daric joined her, as he always did, though he'd long since given up attempting to make conversation. She regretted the necessity of it, especially as she took in his resigned expression.

"Dinner, cottage," said Daric. "If you please." He'd become far more cordial to the home since she'd commented on his directness. The cottage had become more courteous in return.

They served themselves from the assortment of dishes that appeared on the small table. The clink of cutlery on porcelain was the only sound between them. She didn't know how Daric felt, but she could sense the tension building between them like an invisible fortress, suffocating her in loneliness.

"I'm sorry," she said, unable to take the self-imposed silence any longer.

He looked at her, mouth agape and fork paused halfway to his mouth. "For what?"

She shrugged one shoulder, suddenly uncomfortable with his full attention. "For being distant."

"You owe me no apologies. This," he gestured around them, "is a lot to take in. You're entitled to whatever you need to help you process everything. If that means not interacting with me, so be it." His words were casual enough, but she knew he was hurt by her cold treatment.

"Even so, I'm sorry."

He waved her off and finally moved his bite to his mouth, but she couldn't let it go without further explanation.

"When the witch came and things changed, I realized that maybe this isn't the safe haven I thought it was. I–" she swallowed, trying to push down the nerves suddenly threatening to overwhelm her. "I like you and that scares me."

He opened his mouth to speak, but she held up a hand to stop him.

"Please, just let me finish." He nodded and she pressed on, buoyed by his deferment. "You were right when you said I wouldn't always want to be here. I want to break the curse—both of our curses," she added. "But if anything happens, and only one of us is freed, I don't want either of us to feel the hurt of that loss any worse than we have to. I thought keeping you at arm's length was the best thing for both of us."

Daric nodded again, looking thoughtful with his chin propped on his fist. "I will always regret not being close to you if the option is available. It's normal to fear pain, but take it from someone who knows, it's better to feel the pain of loss than to have never felt the joy of love."

Her heart stuttered at that word; the one that had been mocking her all day, the one she feared more than pain, though they seemed destined to coincide. She thought of the way Daric made her feel. The way her breath caught when his skin brushed hers. The way he made her laugh so effortlessly. The way he actually listened when she spoke. He made her feel valued, cherished, and, yes, even loved—but she couldn't accept that it was that simple.

She thought back to his actions, his words, and her eyes widened as she made connections she'd never considered before.

"Your curse," she whispered, but Daric tensed at the words nonetheless. "Am I supposed to fall in love with you?"

He didn't deny it, his pained expression telling her everything she needed to know.

"She stripped you of your title and trapped you in a secluded cottage in the middle of the forest, then tasked you with finding someone who would fall in love with you?" Her voice grew louder with every word, shouting by the end of her tirade.

Unable to speak about his curse, Daric held up his palms and shrugged as if to say, *what can you do?*

Alaine was disgusted. That witch had left him with no way to break the curse for over three hundred years until she'd randomly decided to stick her there as well. If that witch ever dared to show her face again, Alaine would have some strong words for her.

"I was going to leave this for you in the library after you'd gone to bed, but seeing as how you're speaking to me again, I'd really like to see you open it." He rose and crossed the room to the sofa she no longer frequented. Reaching beneath, he pulled out a small wooden box decorated with inlaid roses and twisting vines. He brought it back to the table, setting it before her reverently.

There was a small brass key protruding from a hole on the side closest to her. Tentatively, Alaine reached out and turned the key. The lid opened with a quiet *snick* and she lifted it with trembling fingers. Inside was a sheaf of paper, inkwell, and feather quill. She looked at Daric for answers and he laughed gently at her baffled expression.

"You read so much, I wanted you to have a way to tell your own story." He rubbed the back of his neck, looking sheepish. "I thought it might help you see your worth if you could view yourself from an outsider's perspective."

She brushed her fingers along the side of the box, admiring the contents. Daric was a prince, but somehow he knew the way to her heart could not be paved with gold and jewels. His thoughtfulness made her heart lurch. While she wanted to believe his generosity stemmed from a place of genuine care, she couldn't shake the feeling that his intentions weren't true. Perhaps it was the nature of his curse that weighed on her.

"Why did you give me this?" she asked, afraid to know the answer, but not wanting to be kept in the dark any longer.

His brow creased in confusion. "I've just told you, I thought it would help you break your curse."

She searched his eyes for any sign of duplicity, finding none, but remained unable to rid herself of the feeling of unease. "You had no thoughts for your own curse? Can you honestly look me in the eye and tell me that you didn't give me this so that I would fall in love with you?"

He didn't speak, either because he didn't want to admit it or because the curse held his tongue. Regardless, she'd successfully reminded herself why she couldn't let him in. Her heart was on the line. Even more so if she was just a means to an end.

She shut the box, already turning to leave when his approaching footsteps made her pause. With her back to him, she couldn't see him reach for the box, so she startled when he slid it across the table toward her.

"Please take it. I still want you to have it."

She made a small noise of protest, opening her mouth to argue, but for once he continued without letting her speak.

"I can't promise that I didn't consider your feelings toward me, because a part of me will always hope that you can—" he choked and she knew it was the curse preventing him from speaking. His roar of frustration startled her, but she kept her body angled away from him.

He blew out a frustrated breath and started again. "I'll always hope that you can feel *some way* about me, regardless of whether or not that would free me. But you—you are one of the kindest, smartest, funniest, most selfless people I have ever met and it is so damn frustrating that all you see when you look at yourself is your external beauty."

She turned at his explosive outburst, shocked at the strength of his speech. She nearly jumped back when she saw how close they were. Now that they faced each other, she had to tilt her chin to see the sincerity blazing in his eyes.

"It's true that you're beautiful, but I knew that before the witch returned your face. I'm sorry that I didn't tell you before. I'll regret it every day for the rest of my life, but please don't let my mistakes keep you from freeing yourself. You deserve the world, even if I'm not a part of it."

His fingers brushed hers and she allowed him to take her hand. She expected him to twine their fingers, but instead, he placed her hand over the gift box.

"I hope you learn your value, so that when you are free, you can find a man truly worthy of you."

As his hand slipped from hers, she had the overwhelming sense that this was a turning point. If she let him walk away, she was saying goodbye to whatever future they might have together. Panic seized her at the thought of losing him forever and she realized that she would take whatever pain the future held if it meant a chance for even a few moments of love with Daric.

She grabbed for his hand, pulling him toward her as she wrapped her arms around his neck and planted her lips firmly against his. Whatever resistance he had quickly melted away, his arms encircling her and pulling her flush against his hard body. She gasped at the contact, marveling at the way her supple curves melded to his hard planes. Their tender kiss turned heated as he slid his tongue along her bottom lip. All thoughts of curses and witches disappeared as she opened her lips to him. He groaned into her mouth, bringing his hands up to cup her face, thumbs caressing her cheeks.

He pulled away suddenly and she was surprised to find herself gasping for breath. She was grateful for Daric's hands holding her steady as the world spun around them.

"What's wrong?" he whispered, his voice thick and gravelly.

"What?" She had trouble processing his words through the haze left behind in the wake of their kiss.

"You're crying." He stroked her cheek again and she felt the wetness as he smeared it over her skin.

Alaine didn't know why was crying except that she was scared and nervous and excited and happy. The multitude of emotions overwhelmed her completely and for a moment, there was nothing she could do but stand in his arms and let the tears flow. He held her through it all, demanding nothing of her as his mere presence soothed her soul.

After several moments, the tears subsided. When she finally opened her mouth to speak, it was to give voice to the truth in heart. "I think I love you."

His face lit up with joy and then he was gone.

CHAPTER 26

Daric

It took Daric a moment to recognize where he was. One minute, he'd finally had his lips pressed to Alaine's, her soft, warm body in his arms. The next, he stood in the center of a cavernous room. The cold hit him like plunging into a frozen river. No glass remained in any of the windows, the shattered remains scattered about like glitter. The setting sun illuminated a crumbling fresco adorning the wall across from him, and the once-polished stone floor lay beneath several layers of grime. A maze of cracks wound toward the towering throne in the center of it all.

His throne.

His *home*.

His knees buckled beneath the weight of recognition and he sank to the floor. He was home. He was *free*.

Tears welled at the corner of his eyes, blurring the sight before him into something that more closely resembled the castle of his memories. He felt a sob rising in his chest and pressed a fist to his mouth to contain it. His heart raced as he considered what it meant that he was no longer trapped in that cottage. Not only was he free of the curse and the witch, but Alaine *loved* him, and that fact meant more to him than all the rest.

Her love filled him with renewed purpose, but he'd been spirited away before he could tell her how he felt. Rising, he turned in place, searching the room for her though he already knew in his bones she was not there. He felt her absence as surely as if he'd lost a limb. Like the disappearing sun, the warmth of her embrace had all but left him. He'd feared this chill from the moment he began to love her and now it crept in on a phantom wind, an echo of the cold and distant person he'd been before her. He shivered at the reminder and made a conscious effort to cling to the joy Alaine had shown him.

He longed for her comforting touch as a thorough scan of his surroundings confirmed the remnants of a pilfered castle were all the company he kept. Luckily, whoever now ruled this area had chosen somewhere else to reside.

It was unclear how long the castle had been vacant. Daric had no idea if his family line had ended with him. He'd been unwilling to question Alaine about it, certain his inquiries would only rouse her suspicions. In time, perhaps he'd research the history, learn if his father had chosen another successor or if the crown had been decided by war.

Little remained of the home he'd known beyond the carved wood throne, which was likely too heavy to be plucked up by someone hoping to earn some easy coin. Long shadows spilled over the room, the darkness engulfing him as he sat on the throne. He braced his forearms along the armrests and leaned back, mimicking the position his father had taken many times. As he gazed out at his empty court, Daric felt nothing. Not regret for the king he'd never be; nor sadness for the family he'd mourned centuries before. The castle was a relic, a thing of the past, and his future lay somewhere beyond its walls.

With sudden urgency, he jumped to his feet. "Witch!" he bellowed, feet already moving as he recognized it for the futile pursuit that it was. He knew she would never appear to him in defeat. If he was truly free, then he was rid of her forever. He smiled as he left the throne room behind, hoping she spent the rest of her days miserable and alone as he had done for so long.

If he'd been returned to his home, perhaps Alaine had been returned to hers. He knew the land had changed since he'd been poised to rule over it, but Alaine had spoken of her village, a larger town in the shadow of the forest. He hoped it was the same one he was thinking of, but it was a better start than nothing.

Rushing down a spiraling staircase, he didn't bother to search any more of the crumbling castle, knowing there was nothing more for him here. He hoped he could find a horse or cart nearby willing to take him where he needed to go. With any luck, he'd see Alaine again before the week's end. He didn't care if he had to search the world, he would find her and he would tell her he loved her.

CHAPTER 27

Alaine

A laine blinked and he was gone. Like a figment of her imagination, he vanished without a trace before her very eyes. The only hint that he'd been there at all was the faint tingling sensation in her swollen lips. She waited, expecting to disappear herself, finding only disappointment as her feet remained firmly planted on the cottage floor. It was possible that Daric's curse hadn't been broken. Perhaps the witch had seen their kiss and sought to punish him. She didn't trust the witch to fulfill her end of the bargain when it was clear she'd been toying with them all along.

Frustrations mounting, she kicked out a chair, sending it careening onto its side. She grabbed a plate off the table and threw it against the wall where it shattered on impact. The crash unleashed something inside of her and she swiped the remaining dishes onto the floor. Turning in place, she ripped down curtains, smashed vases, and toppled a small table, demolishing everything in reach. She plucked the gift box off the table and froze with it poised over her head. As much as she wanted to resent the item that led her to this point, she couldn't bring herself to destroy the last thing he'd given her. A sob wracked her body as she clutched it to her chest, trying and failing to fill the hole where Daric had been only minutes earlier.

Though her eyes ached with unshed tears, they refused to fall, building a lump in her throat that she struggled to breathe around. She felt the absence of the words she'd spoken—knew she'd opened herself to this hurt in offering her truth, but she couldn't bring herself to regret any of it. The ghost of Daric's answering smile lingered on the back of her eyelids, the promise of something good if ever she could free herself. A keening wail ripped free from her, taking with it the last reserves of her energy as she collapsed the wreckage.

"Pathetic."

Alaine knew without looking that the witch had appeared. Of course she was there to witness her sundering. She probably savored the taste of her misery like one would a fine wine.

"What have you done?" asked Alaine, piercing the witch with the best glare she could muster through the blur of tears. It was the maiden form that stood before her again, hair gleaming in the firelight as she picked her way through the destruction.

"Me?" The witch placed a hand on her chest, feigning innocence. "I'm sure I don't know what you're talking about." She picked a piece of lint from her shoulder, the picture of apathy as Alaine's world crumbled around her.

"Liar! What have you done to Daric? Where did you take him?"

The witch glared at her outburst, her anger finally piercing through the calm facade. "*I* didn't do anything to him. *You* broke the curse. He's free. He's been returned home." She said this with a mix of disgust and regret, but Alaine had no pity for her.

"And what about me?" Alaine cringed at the pleading tone of her voice, but she would throw herself prostrate before her if it meant being freed, if it gave her a chance to find Daric.

The witch's eyes narrowed. "What about you? *You* haven't fulfilled the terms of your curse. As it stands, you're still mine." She smiled and Alaine's gut twisted.

"This curse is absurd. How can I ever hope to win when you can change the rules anytime you want?"

"It was not I who meddled with the powers at play." The witch's fists clenched at her sides, but her eyes lit with cruel cunning. "Do you want to know what he bargained? Do you want to know what was so important that he practically handed himself over to me?"

Alaine was positive she would rather not know, but the witch didn't wait for an answer.

"He bargained his freedom in exchange for yours. You had one year to fall in love with him or he would give himself over to me, so you could be free."

She didn't know there were pieces of her heart that weren't broken until then.

"Then why am I still here?" Her voice broke, matching the shattered organ in her chest. The hopelessness that had been expelled with Daric's kiss now rebounded tenfold.

"He didn't bargain for you to fall in love with him. The deal was, if you *didn't* love him after a year, you would be free—but you do, so here we are. Both left without our prince."

Rage simmered inside her at the thought of Daric belonging to this witch. Alaine snarled, the feral beast she kept contained for decorum finally breaking free. "Your curse is a joke. You'll not have me any more than you have him. You challenge me to learn my worth? I already know it, because Daric reminded me of it every chance he got." She stood, invading the witch's space and forcing her to retreat as she advanced. "I am smart, but I am open. I am kind, but I am cautious. I am stubborn. I am scared. I am funny, and clever, and lovely, and fierce. I am all the things you will never be, and I am done. Now, free me."

CHAPTER 28

The Witch

T he girl disappeared in the blink of an eye, leaving the witch utterly and completely alone in the enchanted cottage. For the first time in centuries, Eudora existed unaccompanied within her own mind. She felt the weight of the curse lift from her shoulders and with it vanished the otherworldly presence that had possessed her all these years. With Them gone, Eudora felt like a stranger in her body. She was relieved to find that she maintained the form of the maiden she had been before the spell, fearing that she would be freed only to find her body that of the withered crone. After so long sharing the space within her, she didn't know who she was anymore. She'd never imagined becoming entangled for years, let alone centuries.

Once she'd cast the spell, only Daric and the one who loved him could undo it.

A spell to find love.

She thought she'd been clever enough to circumvent natural law. Thought she'd been careful enough with the crafting of the spell, but she'd been young and foolish.

With every passing year, she had felt herself slipping farther away, toward an oblivion that surely would have doomed all three of them. The cost of the magic had been higher than she'd anticipated—more than she could pay if she was honest with herself. She owed her life to the terrible being that stepped into her body like a second skin. They had borne the repercussions in her stead, Their magic fueling the curse long enough for Daric, and later Alaine, to break it. Without Their intervention, Eudora certainly wouldn't have survived.

Though she'd spent most of the past centuries fearing the fickle whims of the being that controlled her body and magic, she remained both grateful to Them and relieved They were gone. She'd been concerned that her recent involvement would push Alaine and Daric too far in the opposite direction, but it was a risk that paid off.

She envied Alaine at that moment, for her surety of self and the confidence she'd projected. Perhaps one day, Eudora would find herself again. Until then, there remained work to be done.

After all that she'd endured, she hadn't had the strength to ensure Alaine and Daric found each other in the aftermath. They'd been freed, yes, but both to their own homes, though luckily in the same time—they wouldn't have to face the devastation that could have been if Daric had been sent back to his own century. It was technically Daric who had set these events into motion, but the curse was entirely Eudora's doing, albeit unintentionally. She intended to make amends, and this time, she'd do it without magic.

Well, without *big* magic, at least.

She only hoped they would be willing to accept her help after everything.

CHAPTER 29

Daric

B y the time Daric reached the grand foyer and pushed his way through the colossal door, the sun had dipped below the distant hills. Night would soon be upon him. His first thought was to check the stables, but he rejected that plan at the sight of the overgrown lawn. No part of this castle had shown any sign of regular maintenance. There was no point searching for a horse when the property had clearly been abandoned.

Though he had no food, no horse, and only a vague idea of where he was heading, his only thoughts were of Alaine.

Had she been freed as well?

Was she home?

Was she safe?

His anxiety spiked as he spiraled into darker thoughts. She could still be at the cottage, alone—or worse, the witch could be tormenting her. Fear quickened his steps until he was sprinting across the unkempt lawns, brushing aside overgrown shrubs and leaping over fallen trees. It had been so long since he'd had the room to run and even his adrenaline was not enough to mask the burning in his lungs or the pain in his side.

Still, he ran.

He didn't spare a backward glance for the castle. Prince Daric was no more. He was only Daric, the beast of the enchanted cottage, a man in love. And he would stop at nothing to find her again.

His fingers and toes had grown numb by the time the flicker of lantern light indicated he neared a small town. He would have sighed in relief at the sign of life if he'd had any breath to spare. As it was, he barely managed to hold himself upright as he passed by several wattle and daub homes, their windows already dark for the evening. Eventually, the tiny path opened up into a large avenue and small homes gave way to larger structures of wood and stone.

Though the sun had set, there were still several people milling about the town. Daric finally slowed to a stop before a bustling inn and tavern. His legs rebelled against the lack of motion, urging him forward even as they seemed to weigh ten stones each. The itch of his blood rushing through his body nearly drove him mad. A couple patrons lingering outside gave him questioning looks as he fought to catch his breath, but most were too absorbed in their own business to pay him any mind.

It shocked him to see so many other people. For hundreds of years, he'd seen only the witch when she deigned to show herself. Then for the last couple of months, he'd had Alaine. But the handful of people he could see now nearly immobilized him. He had to close his eyes and remind himself that this was the real world.

The smell of roast meat and beer wafted out from the tavern, the raucous noise that accompanied it counteracting the effect of the enticing scent. His stomach begged him to stop and replenish his energy, but he hesitated at the door weighing his need for nourishment against his desire to continue moving. Under the curse, he'd eaten only out of habit, a semblance of normalcy he'd clung to in the absence of necessity. Now, his hunger gnawed at him, encouraging him to stray from his task. Though he was almost certain he knew the town Alaine had referred to in her stories, she had called it by another name and it was enough to make him doubt his conviction. However, with no money or items to barter, he'd be hard-pressed to acquire food through any lawful means. It also meant he'd be unlikely to find the answer he sought within.

In the end, his empty purse decided his path and he darted around back to the stables, pausing at a well to quench his thirst and splash some water on his brow. The freezing water shocked his tired mind to alertness and filled his belly enough to stave off the worst of the hunger pangs.

With his head cleared, he entered the small stable, surprised—or maybe lucky—to find no stablehands in sight. Despite the lack of attendants, the stable smelled better than he expected. He noticed only a faint scent of hay and leather as he slunk down the aisle, checking each of the stalls as he passed. It was possible there were no horses here after all. That would have accounted for the lack of smell and attendants.

He started to think his detour had been a waste of time when he finally located the only horse in the stable; a chestnut mare that barely spared him a glance between bites of hay. It seemed fate was on his side since she was still saddled, but Daric also knew that meant her rider might not be long away.

Moving quickly, he unlatched the stall door, wincing at the squeal of rusty hinges as it swung out towards him. The mare paid him little heed as he entered, but he held out his hands and murmured calming sounds to keep from spooking her. Though she was saddled, the bridle still hung on the wall. It wasn't until he lifted it from the small metal hook that the mare showed any reaction at all. Suddenly, either at the prospect of being bridled or being bridled by a stranger, the mare skittered back, pressing against the wall opposite him, her ears pinned back as she stamped and whinnied.

The last thing Daric wanted was a scared horse when it had been well over three hundred years since he'd last been astride one. Though he'd been a decent rider at the time, years out of practice had made him wary. He'd be damned if he had to search the town for another horse though. Time moved on and every second that ticked by was a second he could spend searching for Alaine. In the end, his fear for her overrode his trepidation and he surged the animal.

He instantly regretted ignoring years of training and his own instincts when the mare reared up. The last thing he saw was the hoof careening toward his face before a bolt of agony knocked him out cold.

CHAPTER 30

Alaine

Alaine startled awake with no recollection of having fallen asleep. Apparently, she had made it to bed; its soft embrace beckoned her back to sleep even as she fought against it. She forced herself upright, willing the fog of sleep from her mind so she could make sense of what had happened the night before. She remembered telling Daric that she loved him, his subsequent disappearance, and demanding that the witch free her too, but everything after was a blur. Between then and now, the hours had stretched until it felt like days had passed since he'd gone.

The gloomy interior of her bedroom matched her sour mood, but she'd never known it to be this dark in the cottage before. She thought it might still be night, although it was more likely Daric had taken the light with him when he left. Hope had abandoned her and she remained a hollow husk of the vibrant girl she'd been with him.

Despite the emptiness, her limbs were heavy as she swung her legs over the side of the bed. She slid off, surprised to find solid wood beneath her feet.

"Did you change my room again, cottage?" she called out, wincing at the volume of her voice as it echoed back to her. She hoped that wherever Daric had ended up, he was enjoying his freedom more than she was her solitude. "I'd like the old rug back, if I may."

Just then, the sound of hurried footsteps approached her closed door.

"Daric?" His name was on her lips before she could squash the hope that built in her chest. She raced to the door, or she tried to, running into various pieces of furniture that hadn't been there before. Something fell, shattering on the floor, the sound jarring in the small space.

Sunlight poured in as the door opened, freezing her in place while momentarily blinded by the brightness.

"Alaine."

She heard her name and arms wrapped around her, but the voice was too high, the arms too small. Confused, she flinched away, blinking rapidly until her vision could adjust to the brightness.

Before her stood her mother, her father lingering in the doorway, relief painting both of their faces.

"Mother? Father?" Her brain refused to put the pieces together. *Had the witch actually freed her?* "What happened? Where's Daric?"

Her parents exchanged blank looks.

"Alaine, darling," said her mother, reaching for her once again. Alaine allowed herself to be captured for now. "You've been unconscious for weeks."

Alaine's heart stopped. *Unconscious? For weeks?*

She must have looked as shocked as she felt. Her mother began stroking her arms, continuing to explain as though her world had not just imploded.

"We didn't know what happened. The doctor said you must have sustained a head injury. Alaine, darling, why didn't you tell us you'd been hurt? We've been worried sick."

"I–" She touched the back of her head gingerly, remembering the force of the blow as Baxter had pushed her back. "I've been here the whole time?"

She looked to her father for confirmation, hating that the pity in his eyes confirmed her fears. She couldn't believe none of it had been real.

"I had just told you about Lord Baxter's offer when you fainted." Though his words were gentle, her father's artfully composed expression suggested there was more that he wasn't saying. "We thought it was the shock of the marriage at first, but then you didn't recover and I knew something was wrong." His fingers turned bone white from wringing them and Alaine wondered if it was guilt his careful mask concealed.

"That's not right, though," Alaine begged. "I left. I went to the forest. I've been gone for weeks." Her eyes burned with unshed tears.

"Oh, don't cry, dear. You're too pretty to cry." Her mother's face assumed her usual look of scorn as she fussed over her. "I understand this must be confusing for you, but Lord Baxter is here. He's come by every day to check on you. We were visiting with him just now when we heard you stirring. I expect he'll want to see you if you're feeling up to it. It's about time we finalize this wedding contract."

"But Daric—"

"No buts," her mother interjected. "I don't know who this Daric fellow is, but you'll hold your tongue in front of Lord Baxter. You're lucky he's been so loyal. Any other man would have found himself a different bride after so many weeks. Patience of a saint, that one."

"I've only just awoken. Surely, this can wait for another day?"

"That's enough of that. I've told you already, he's been a patient man, but we don't want today to be the day that patience runs out. I'm sure he knows you're awake by now. It would be rude to keep him waiting."

Her mother prattled on, but the words flew in one ear and out the other. Alaine was home. She had always been home. There was no witch, no cottage, and no Daric. She would marry Lord Baxter and save her family. And she would never again feel the joy she'd known in the moments before waking.

"I'm sorry."

She meant the words that slipped from her mouth, but she wasn't apologizing to her mother. She was sorry she'd let herself be swept away by some fever dream. Sorry that she'd unwittingly fallen in love with a figment of her imagination—a fictional hero she'd assembled from all her favorite characters. Sorry that she'd regained consciousness to find it had all been a lie when it had seemed so real.

She let her mother dress her like she was a child again. There was no time for a proper bath with Baxter waiting downstairs. Her mother pinned her hair back with quick efficiency, tucking most of it into a bonnet that she said *would have to do*. Alaine didn't help. She let herself be trussed up like a prize chicken, even knowing she was about to be fed to the wolf.

The minutes ticked by too quickly and soon it was time to face the man who had hunted, threatened, and abused her. The man who would be her husband. And even though he wasn't real, she regretted every second she'd taken for granted with Daric.

She would treasure those moments lost in a dream world for the rest of her life and hope that she would return one day.

CHAPTER 31

Daric

Daric woke to a blinding headache and the cool sting of iron around his wrists. He tried opening his eyes and discovered one was swollen shut, the skin around it hot with fever. When he prodded it, his fingers met a thick layer of salve as though someone had thought to patch him up before clapping him in irons. He lay on a cold, unforgiving surface, his muscles and joints protesting as he rolled to his side. The icy floor was soothing to his inflamed face at least. From what he could tell through one eye in the low light, he guessed he was in a cellar of some sort. There appeared to be several crates and barrels stacked along the opposite wall, and a set of stairs leading up to his right.

He pushed himself upright, bracing his back against the wall as a wave of nausea hit him. Luckily, he hadn't eaten recently, so there wasn't much to come back up. However, he didn't fancy the notion of smelling vomit for however long he was to be trapped here. He took several deep breaths until his stomach settled, knowing he would need all his strength if he stood any chance of escaping.

In the dark, he felt along each of the manacles, testing for weakness and finding none. They'd been looped around a support post and Daric didn't trust the structure to stay standing if he tried to sever it. As a last resort, he could break his hand to be free, but he'd wait until he could learn if the door at the top of the stairs was unlocked. He would fight his way out if needed, though his injury might prove problematic.

The door opened above and a beam of light speared across the room. Daric noted there'd been no sound of a key turning, which likely meant an unlocked door. A figure stepped into the light, a man it seemed, but Daric could make out nothing against the blinding sunlight.

His hand stopped halfway to shielding his eyes, the action cut short by the chains he'd already forgotten.

The man left the door open behind him as he descended the stairs. The fool.

Daric was almost insulted at being captured by this careless man, but then he remembered he had been knocked unconscious by a horse. That would have made him considerably easier to apprehend.

Hoping to lean on the stranger's apparent naivety, Daric let his head fall to one side, slackened his arms, and sprawled his legs apart to appear as helpless as possible.

"You're not fooling me." The voice resonating from the man was deep and confident as he reached the foot of the stairs.

The faint sound of flint on steel preceded a small flame lighting a lantern. He held it aloft, illuminating a face that appeared chiseled from stone. A proud nose and brow were complimented by full lips and kind eyes, all framed by a chiseled jaw and cheekbones. With a straight back and solid frame, he radiated humble confidence.

Daric refused to blink away from the flames reflecting in the man's ebony eyes as he stalked closer.

He stopped just out of Daric's reach and kicked at his booted foot.

"I told you, you're not fooling me." The man squatted so they were at eye level, holding the lantern up so Daric had to squint his good eye. "Daisy didn't hit you nearly as hard as she could have."

Daisy must have been the mare he'd tried to steal. If this man was half as clever as his horse—or as violent—Daric might have some trouble escaping after all.

He remained silent, curious why he'd been locked in a cellar rather than arrested on sight as most would have done.

"Don't you speak?" the man asked. No cruelty laced his words, only mere curiosity.

Daric weighed his options. He could feign incomprehension, but then the man might call on the authorities. If he spoke, the man would want answers and, while he no longer felt the gag of the curse holding back, he didn't know how much he should share with a complete stranger.

"Aye, I can speak." His voice was hoarse, a mere whisper compared to the man across from him.

He raised a single eyebrow in response. "All right, I'm listening." The man sat cross-legged just out of reach of Daric's feet, as though he was settling in for a long story.

Again, Daric contemplated how much of his story to reveal. How much would be necessary to see him freed? He debated lying, concocting an elaborate ruse to convince this fellow that he deserved to be let go, but the pain in his head impeded his creativity. In the end, he settled for the truth or as much of the truth as he was willing to share.

"I find myself in a desperate hurry to reach the town of Maribonne."

The man canted his head but said nothing as he regarded Daric, his dark eyes demanding further explanation without words.

The silence stretched between them until Daric exhaled a long breath. He supposed he owed this man more of an explanation after trying to steal his horse.

"I believe that the woman I love may be there and I fear—" he stopped, unwilling to speak that which urged his feet forward. "I fear that there are forces at work keeping us apart. I will not rest until she is in my arms again."

"Ah," the stranger held up one finger to stop him, "but you have already rested, courtesy of my horse."

Daric glared in response. "I apologize for the attempted thievery. What is it you require as recompense?" He was eager to be gone and would likely promise this man all the riches he did not have if it meant getting to Alaine.

"I would have you know the truth, Prince Daric."

Daric startled at the voice that had plagued his nightmares coming from the man before him, the sound so at odds with what he saw.

"It's not possible." The words slipped from his mouth as it opened in shock. Try as he might, he couldn't wrap his brain around the idea of the witch being there. He refused to believe he was still trapped in that curse or worse, that he had been freed and somehow she'd ensnared him again.

Horror froze the blood in his veins as he watched the face before him twist and morph into that of the red-haired witch he knew so well. That chill quickly turned to fire as three hundred years of rage ignited within him. If she had come to claim him again, he would not succumb without a fight. For the first time in centuries, Daric had a reason to live—the *desire* to live. He would not lose his one chance at love and freedom.

He clambered to his feet, bracing his hands on his thighs as he waited for the room to stop spinning. The witch rose with him and he resisted the urge to flinch from her outstretched hand. He let her inch closer, feeling his muscles tense like an adder waiting to strike. Ignoring the shock that occurred as her fingers made contact with the swollen side of his face, Daric seized her wrist, spinning her as he pulled her back flat against his chest. He held her arm immobilized across her chest, his chains pressing precariously against her throat.

For a moment, he reveled in the feel of her struggling in his grasp, the utter helplessness of a fly caught in a web. Revulsion quickly followed in its wake. Never before had he felt joy at another's pain. He wouldn't become that man, but he would do whatever was necessary to see Alaine safe. There would be no pride in her spilling blood, but neither would he feel shame for finding that peace.

The witch's lips were moving, though Daric permitted her no air to give them sound. He could not give her a chance to cast her dark magic. With one arm holding her in place, he batted away her hands as she clawed at his face, her touch little more than the flutter of fingers over his injury.

No—that wasn't right.

He'd noted the shock of their connection at first but ignored the continued sparks that *zinged* across his face as she touched him. They tingled and itched like a wound recently scabbed. With each touch, the pain in his head subsided and the pulsing heat of fever calmed. He sensed his face return to normal and hesitantly blinked his right eye open. The witch slipped from his grasp as his hold on the chains slackened in surprise.

"I mean you no harm," the witch rasped, the words barely loud enough to reach his ear a breath away. "I simply came to explain. It's time you knew the truth."

Daric warred with himself. He had no reason to trust the witch, but something deep within told him to listen.

"You want to talk? Fine. But we will do so as civilized individuals. Give me your word that you will release me from these chains and speak to me as an equal, or I will end you where you stand." Though he tamped down his fury, his voice was little more than a growl.

"I swear it."

With a small key she procured from some hidden pocket, the witch unlocked the manacles around his wrists. As the chains landed on the floor with a resounding *clang*, Daric felt lighter in more ways than one. He expected the witch to conjure a table and chairs as well, but she selected a pair of overturned crates and sat unceremoniously, rubbing her neck where the chain had bitten it.

Daric considered standing, grateful to have the upper hand for once, but the agreement had been for them to come together as equals. He nudged the remaining crate away from the witch before lowering himself to her level. She smirked despite the bruises forming on her throat.

"Can't you heal that too?" he asked out of honest curiosity.

Her knowing look said that she expected the question, but she answered anyway. "All magic comes with a cost. I've just healed you. It will be some time before I can do the same for myself."

Daric accepted her vague answer, eager to be done with the conversation. "You mentioned wanting me to know the truth.

The truth about what?" He hoped he would not regret leaving her alive when he'd had the chance to end her.

"The truth about your so-called curse and why it was your doing, not mine."

CHAPTER 32

Alaine

Lord Henrik Baxter looked just as Alaine remembered him, not a hair out of place as he lounged at the head of their table. Boots propped on a neighboring chair and arms crossed, he exuded haughty boredom, not even bothering to rise as she made her way toward him.

His greedy eyes roved over her body, no doubt ensuring the goods he'd waited so long for remained untampered. She kept her head high, refusing to cower in his presence. If he thought he was getting a rose, she'd make sure to sharpen her thorns.

"My dear Alaine." She flinched at her name from his lips. Having grown accustomed to the natural way it had rolled off Daric's tongue, Baxter's bite sounded jarring by comparison. "It is so good to see you awake and well."

His saccharine words rang false to her ears, but she plastered on a fake smile to appease her parents as they took up positions on either side of her. Rather than bolstering her confidence, they stood like sentries, caging her in, though she'd already accepted her fate. Her fever dreams had been wildly vivid, but even if it had all actually happened, she'd make the same choice. She would do this. For her family, she would do this.

"I am grateful for your patience, and for the assistance you have offered my family." She wanted to spit in his face and claw his eyes out, to mark him so savagely that his outward appearance reflected the physical and emotional pain he'd inflicted on her. Instead, she folded her hands demurely and waited for her father to pull out her chair.

She stared at Baxter's polished, black boots on the chair between them as she sat. Sunlight glinted off their shining surface, yet another piece of his carefully constructed image.

There would come a day when no amount of polishing could restore the youthful beauty she now possessed. She wondered if Baxter considered that far in the future if he had plans for her once she served her purpose. Perhaps he'd simply find another shiny victim. She would look forward to the day she'd be cast aside. Her freedom was only twenty, maybe thirty years away.

Neither of her parents looked her way as they took seats at the opposite end of the table. She couldn't recall missing them in her dreams, but maybe her mind had always known she was home in bed. She didn't think she would miss them once she married—her father perhaps, but not her mother. Resentment bubbled up inside of her where she'd expected guilt. It surprised her enough that she almost cried out, spewing the hurtful words that lined up on her tongue.

She choked them down along with the excuses she wanted to make for them. Yes, she would do her duty to her family and marry Lord Baxter, but she would be damn angry about it.

"I think it's about time we get the business of this marriage underway." Baxter dismissed Alaine completely, turning to address her parents as though she had no say in the matter.

Her mother nodded emphatically.

"That seems wise," her father said, wringing his hands on the table before him.

Baxter took a healthy swig from the glass of wine before him. "I've had the contract written. My man will deliver it in the morrow. We can wed before midday."

"No." All eyes turned to Alaine, varying degrees of shock on each of their faces. She hadn't meant to disagree but saw no point in taking it back now. "It would seem that I have suffered from a tremendous ordeal. I think it prudent to allow me some time to recuperate before the excitement of a wedding." The look of disgust on Baxter's face bolstered her confidence. "Our original agreement was to wed by the first snowfall of the season. I will honor that and marry you as the first flakes fall from the sky."

There was no way to know how soon that day would come. She could wake tomorrow to the crisp taste of frost in the air, but hopefully, nature would be on her side. Surely everything would seem much more manageable after a few days to wrap her head around it. She still held out hope that she would find another way out of this mess, but she'd lost too much time while unconscious.

Baxter looked like he wished to explode out of his seat. Alaine expected steam to spurt from his ears at any moment.

Surprisingly, her mother stepped in to defend her. "That would give us some time to make the necessary arrangements. We'll need to alter your dress and prepare your belongings to be transported to the Lord's manor."

"I suppose that will do," Baxter acquiesced, albeit grudgingly if the look on his face was any indication. He swallowed back the last of his drink and shoved away from the table, boots thudding as his feet dropped to the floor. "Might I speak to my betrothed alone?"

Alaine looked to her parents, hoping her face conveyed the full scope of her horror at the prospect of being alone with him, but they didn't even glance her way as they rose to leave. Baxter's gaze, however, was a constant searing heat on the side of her face. He was a fox in the hen house, but Alaine was no spring chicken.

She bit her lip to keep from calling after her parents, knowing it would be in vain. They had invited the fox in, after all. It was an effort to maintain her unconcerned façade as the door closed behind them. She clasped her hands below the table to hide their trembling.

Caged in, she heard only the pounding of her heartbeat, like a clock ticking down her last moments of freedom.

The air shifted as Baxter stood and she crossed her arms over her chest reflexively.

He huffed a derisive laugh. His steps were calm and measured as he walked toward her, contrary to the erratic beating in her chest. "They'll be mine eventually."

"What will?" She hated that her voice came out breathy and cleared her throat as he halted behind her.

His breath on her cheek was the only warning before he whispered in her ear. "Every part of you."

A jolt ran down her spine and she tensed at his close proximity. He ran a possessive hand from her shoulder to the front of her neck, his fingers lingering on the exposed skin below her collarbone before coming to rest against her throat. His grip was firm enough to hold her in place but gentle enough that it wouldn't leave a mark, his pressure so accurate she wondered how many times he had used this particular maneuver.

Revulsion turned her stomach like spoiled milk. She closed her eyes against the nausea that followed his touch, at once grateful she'd been offered no food or refreshment since waking.

His stubble scratched her cheek as he pressed his face against hers.

"You may run from me, but you can't hide from the snow." He spoke in hushed tones only she could hear. "Don't forget—I'm the only thing standing between your parents and a brutal winter in the cold. Fight me all you want, but I will have you one day, and I'll enjoy making you beg for forgiveness."

She loosed a breath as he released her, catching it again with a gasp as she felt his tongue against her cheek. Shock and disgust hit her so quickly, she fell off the chair as she recoiled from him.

His bellowing laugh seemed to echo as he walked out the door.

CHAPTER 33

Daric

Viewing the witch as an ally proved a difficult task for Daric. He couldn't help but keep her at arm's length, even as they sat on side-by-side crates. However, without the haze of anger and pain clouding his vision, he could truly appreciate the subtle differences in her appearance and demeanor. The edges of her mouth tilted up and her brows lifted slightly; even her teeth lacked the foul color of decay. Her posture was relaxed and non-threatening.

He motioned for her to begin and a look of fear passed across her face as she hesitated.

"I am willing to suspend all judgment until you speak your piece. I'll not harm you, witch."

She smiled and looked down at her hands as she fussed with the edge of her cape. "My name is Eudora." Her eyes flicked up to gauge his reaction, but he made sure to keep his expression neutral. "You might not even remember, but on the day before we first met, you made a wish."

He nodded; he did remember. He had wished for a love as true as the rose and as unrelenting as the seasons. His mind conjured an image of Alaine and he felt his panic rise again.

"Please, before you go on, tell me she is safe. Alaine—is she free?" He would plead if he needed. Not knowing was eating away at his sanity. He wasn't sure he could physically restrain himself long enough to hear her tale without ensuring Alaine's safety.

"She is safe enough. And yes, she freed herself—quite impressively, I might add. You would have been proud to see it."

She was right. Inside he beamed at the thought of Alaine breaking her curse. He'd always known her capable—knew that perhaps she refrained from doing so just to remain there with him—but he would have given anything to see her in action.

"You wished for a love and I brought you one," she said matter-of-factly. "Of course, I had no idea how long it would take to fulfill your wish, nor the cost of the magic. It was too great for me to accomplish on my own. I've spent the entire length of your curse caged within my own body while another—a being of far greater power—possessed me. In the freeing of yourself and Alaine, I have been freed as well. For my part in your suffering, I am sorry. I was foolish to attempt such magic. One cannot expect to throw a rock in a pond and not cause a ripple. A wish like that requires great magic, and magic *always* demands a sacrifice."

"Who was this being?"

"You'd think after sharing a body for so long, I'd have a better idea, but I don't know. They felt *other*, like something so ancient and foreign I wouldn't know how to put a name to what They are."

Daric considered this new information. "Where is this almighty being now?" If what the witch said was true, then his true enemy remained at large.

"Scattered on the breeze or wherever They choose to exist."

Daric felt the instinct to look over his shoulder and check every shadow for a disembodied entity. "You do not fear Their return?"

The witch hummed thoughtfully. "They do not suffer emotions the same way as you and I. They are neither malicious nor benevolent, vengeful or kind. They act and They do not. I believe They are done acting upon us. You and I are a mere grain of sand in the hourglass of Their life."

Though he remained skeptical of her assessment, he had more pressing questions. "People must make wishes all the time. Why me? Why that wish?" He remembered the vibrant colors of autumn at odds with the dying rose as he cast his wish, but the day had been no different than that of previous years. He'd held no talisman, whispered no magic phrase.

She shrugged and waved away his questions with the flick of a wrist. "It was circumstantial. I happened to be listening when the wind whispered your wish. When I followed the threads to a prince with a pure heart, I took a chance."

"You suffered a magical possession and lost over three hundred years of your life on a *chance*?"

"All in the name of love." She winked and it hit him how deeply she'd been altered by the curse's magic. If she was to be believed, the curse had affected her as much as it had him and Alaine, possibly more so. He was glad that she seemed happier, lighter.

"I require one more truth from you." He leaned forward and marked the moment in his mind as the first he approached her without hostile intent.

The witch—Eudora—cocked an eyebrow.

"Where is Alaine?"

She looked away, shame painting her features for the first time since they sat. "She is where you expect her to be, preparing to do what you fear she will do."

"Then, I must make haste." Jumping to his feet, his fingers itched to take up arms, to prepare, to fight, but he had nothing. Nothing beyond a purpose and general direction, but it would have to be enough.

"Wait! There is more you must know, more the magic has taken."

"What more can there be?"

"Alaine remembers your time together, but her town has no memory of her being gone. They believe she hit her head and fell ill. Even her parents think they have been caring for her these past months."

"Your point?" His patience was wearing thin with these delays.

"Her mother *may* have convinced her that you were a fever dream. She is following through with her engagement to Lord Baxter."

Daric closed his eyes, momentarily overwhelmed by the rage building inside him. The collateral damage of a single wish had extended far beyond what he could have imagined. He had been a selfish fool to wish for love. Now, a choice lay before him. Should he pursue the love of his life, saving her from a loveless marriage with nothing to offer in return but his undying affection? Or should he let her go, allowing her to believe him nothing more than a dream while her husband sees to her every need? He would do it. He would step away if he knew for certain that she'd be better off without him.

"She doesn't love him?" He'd meant it as a statement, but his insecurities cast the simple phrase into doubt.

"No, she doesn't."

"I have lost my title, my kingdom, and everything I owned. I am not a man of property. I'm not even a man of this century. Tell me, please, would she be better off with this other man?" He held his hands out, displaying everything he had.

Her smile turned sad. "I cannot tell you that. It is impossible for even me to know."

"Can you restore me to my throne?"

Eudora pursed her lips. "It is technically within my power to do so. However—" she cut him off before he could speak. "The cost would be astronomical. Not only for you and me. The current monarch would need to be deposed, in addition to the consequent removal of all those in line for the throne. Or I would need to wipe the memory of all who know of the current royal family. That's not even considering the price the magic would demand. You would have your kingdom, and by all accounts your love, but at what cost?"

He couldn't tell if it was his own self-pity reflected in her eyes or if she truly felt sorry for him. But he did know that he couldn't take the decision away from Alaine. This love between them was as much hers as it was his, and he refused to make the choice for both of them. He needed to talk to her.

"How do I get to Alaine?"

Chapter 34

Alaine

Days passed in a blur and, before she knew it, Alaine was stepping into the wedding dress her mother had selected. The pale blue brocade was perfect for a winter wedding—or so her mother told her as she repeatedly pinned and prodded the garment. It would need to be taken in as they had assumed, but also hemmed because Alaine refused to wear anything but her fur-lined boots in the snow, much to her mother's chagrin.

"I'm not wearing heeled shoes in the snow. No one will see my feet anyway," Alaine insisted.

Her mother only huffed and stuck her with a pin.

Alaine stared at the bare branches of the tree outside her bedroom window. Winter had arrived and snow would soon follow. She prayed every night for it to hold off for one more day. Thus far, her prayers had been answered, but each day the evening frost lingered a little longer in the morning sun. It was only a matter of time before the clouds overhead brought the dreadful white powder to her doorstep.

"What kind of person sets an event to align with the weather?" Alaine didn't mean to speak the words aloud, but she'd been speaking her mind more frequently since she had nothing left to lose.

"As I recall, it was you who set the date of the nuptials," her mother replied dryly.

"Only because that was the original term of the agreement." She knew she sounded more like a petulant child than a woman about to be married, but the wait was driving her mad. She wanted it to snow already and simultaneously wanted it never to snow again. There was so much to do and nothing that could be done. She felt stretched thin. This odd liminal time left her bereft and irritable, which was no way to begin a new chapter of her life—even one she was already dreading.

Her mother had ceased her fussing and stepped back to admire the dress. Though Alaine felt the gaze upon her, she found no words for the woman who cared so little about her own daughter's happiness.

They stood in silence, the air thick with unspoken words. Minutes passed with Alaine willing her mother to say something—anything—to ease this infernal melancholy. When at last Alaine lifted her gaze to meet her mother's, she knew by their silver-lined edges that she would not find pity or remorse within. Her mother's tears were not those of a woman losing a daughter, but rather tears of joy and pride for the bride-to-be.

Alaine would relish the look on her mother's face if it had been for any reason other than her future marriage to Baxter. Disgusted, she turned her back, presenting the myriad of buttons. In this way at least, her mother freed her from her confines, her deft fingers making quick work of the small fasteners.

The heavy brocade slipped from her shoulders like water pooling at her feet. Alaine all but jumped out of the fabric, half afraid of drowning in it. She shivered in her underdress and pulled on a robe as her mother gingerly picked up the dress, careful to avoid the pins.

Her mother was almost to the door when she stopped and twisted to look over her shoulder at Alaine. "If you find yourself in need of something to do, you can write to your uncle and cousins in North Embrook. They were quite worried for you and I'm sure they'd love to know of your recovery." She turned on her heel without waiting for a reply.

Alaine closed the door behind her, savoring the time to herself. While she wanted to pick up a book and get lost in another world, guilt nagged at her and she eventually acquiesced to writing her family in the north. She did not wish them to worry further on her account.

She sat at her writing desk and folded down the front panel to reveal a flat writing surface and several drawers and compartments. The largest of the drawers opened easily with a slight pull on the small brass handle. Inside lay a wooden stationery box, several old quills, and an ink well.

She pulled the box free and gasped as sunlight revealed the familiar contours of the lid. Her fingers traced over the design even as her mind refused to accept what her eyes were seeing, for inlaid on the lid of the box was a rose she thought existed only in her dreams. Through touch, she confirmed what she feared to be true, that this was indeed Daric's gift from their last day together. How it had come to be in her writing desk, she did not know, but a bolt of panic shot through her at the realization. Because if this was real, then it was all real, and she wasn't ready to accept the fact that Daric might be out there somewhere, looking for her, while she prepared to marry another.

With speed she didn't know she possessed, Alaine flung off her robe and donned the closest overdress she could find. She slipped on her fur-lined boots and grabbed her winter cloak as she sprinted from the room.

The commotion she made as she descended the stairs surely alerted everyone in the house to her departure, but she paid no mind to the shouts that echoed after her as she greeted the cold winter day.

An overcast, gray sky mirrored her mood as the bitter wind nipped at her nose and ears. Dead grass crunched beneath her feet, the mottled landscape blurring as she focused on the towering trees in the distance. She stumbled along, willing her feet faster as they caught in her skirts, and refused to slow until her lungs screamed for air. Even then, she pushed on.

When she finally broke through the tree line, her sides ached and her lungs burned. Her chest and underarms were damp with sweat, a stark contrast to the chill that caused her breath to fog with every exhale. She'd lost feeling in her face and blew into her hands in an attempt to warm them.

Enough foliage remained between the evergreens and the underbrush that the forest appeared dark and foreboding, the leafless trees standing bare like skeleton sentinels throughout.

When she'd entered the forest months ago, it had felt like a homecoming, like she had finally answered a call that had beckoned her for years. Now, it took everything in her not to turn tail and run back to her warm bed—but she had come for a purpose.

She crept forward with tentative steps, the sound swallowed by the leaf-strewn floor, while she looked for the exact spot from her memory. She knew she hadn't been far into the forest, but everything looked different under the blanket of fallen leaves.

At last, she thought she recognized the tree and sank to the ground before it. Her dress instantly soaked through where she knelt in the damp leaves, the cold seeping through to her bones. She shivered and clenched her jaw to keep her teeth from chattering as she sifted through the ground cover. Slowly, with maddening calm, she unearthed a pair of shoes and a book.

Her shoes.

Her book.

Alaine remembered laying those items aside when she first journeyed into the forest. That they were still here meant that not only had she entered the forest, but she hadn't returned to claim them.

She sat back on her heels and hung her head, unsure of what to do with this new information. Not only was everything she remembered true, but no one else knew she had ever been gone. If she had to guess, she'd wager a fair sum that this was still the curse at work. She couldn't be certain she'd broken the curse. After all, just because she'd been freed did not mean the game had ended. She wouldn't be surprised if the witch showed up here, appearing at her lowest moment to bring her lower still.

"Alaine."

Her name was a benediction, so quiet it was almost lost to the wind. She'd been wrong when she thought the witch would be her breaking, for when she turned and saw Daric, standing like a ghost of a memory, she couldn't hold back the flood of tears.

Chapter 35

Daric

He'd caught sight of her as she flew across the open fields, the only streak of color among the somber landscape. Seeing her after so long apart had made his breath catch. He'd lived centuries without her in his life, but these last few days had been the worst sort of torture. Once, they had spoken on the difference between the pain of losing love and that of never experiencing it. Looking back at the agony he'd felt at being torn from her grasp, he wasn't sure he could make the same assertion he had then. Now that he'd found her, he hoped to never feel that kind of pain again, though he still planned to leave the decision in her hands.

She entered the forest without hesitation and he released the breath he'd been holding, the air forming a small cloud before him. He'd been haunting these woods for hours and had lost all feeling in his extremities. Though his feet resisted at first, he crept after her, curious to see what had brought her so quickly to this particular spot. His mind provided endless answers as he followed, each more concerning than the last. She was running from her betrothal. She'd been cast out. She'd been hurt.

His blood started to boil at the possibilities and he fought to reign in his emotions. From the moment she'd stumbled into his garden, he'd been completely helpless for her. It was no less true now as he followed her through the cold, dark woods like a lost puppy.

It had been Eudora's idea to bring him to the forest by Alaine's village. "She will come to you," the witch had said. "Do not seek her out. When she's ready, she will find you."

She'd been at least half right, he guessed. Alaine had come, though he didn't think it was him she was looking for at the base of a towering Aspen.

Daric stood several paces away when she suddenly sank back on the damp ground, curling in on herself as she clutched something in her hands. She made no sound, but his muscles tensed, alerted by her sudden distress signal. It was all the motivation he needed.

"Alaine." Her name rolled off his tongue and he poured every emotion he had into those two syllables.

He didn't know what he'd expected, but her torrent of tears shocked him so completely that he stood motionless for several breaths before rushing to her side. She flinched as his hand met her back and he pulled away, gutted by her response.

"Alaine?" His pulse quickened as she refused to meet his eyes. "What's wrong? Are you hurt?"

It took everything in him not to wrap her in his arms and pull her tight to him, but he dared not after her initial reaction. Perhaps something had happened in their days apart. As though sensing the direction of his thoughts, she slowly edged away. He reached for her reflexively, scared to let the distance between them grow.

"Don't touch me," she whispered, finally meeting his gaze with her own tear-streaked one.

His hand still hovered, frozen, though it had nothing to do with the chill air. He lowered it cautiously, afraid to startle her, and took a couple of steps back for good measure.

"Alaine," he tried again. "It's me, Daric."

"Why are you here?" she hissed out. She took an aggressive step toward him, the wounded animal prepared to fight.

"I came to find you. I thought—" He trailed off, unsure what he had thought. That they could start again where they had left off? That he could inject himself into her life and upset all the plans she had made without knowledge of his existence? He felt like a fool. "I needed to see that you were safe, for myself." A true enough answer, he decided.

"Well, as you can see, I'm quite well," she said, gesturing to her wet and muddy clothes. "Thank you for checking. You may be on your way now."

Daric didn't understand. This was not the Alaine that he knew and loved. Something had changed and he didn't know how to fix it. At a loss for how to proceed with this altered version, he simply waited, giving her space and watching for any hint of the woman he knew within.

They stared at each other, their breath clouding the space between them.

His arms hung limp at his sides, but he raised his chin and let her see him, let her see all of him. Every scar and broken piece, but also the hope and desire he knew radiated from him because of her.

Her head began swinging back and forth, barely perceptible at first and then with fervor. "No," she said. "No, no, no, no, no."

Keeping the distance between them, he squatted, so he might be closer to her level as she sat on the ground. "No what, Alaine?"

She closed her eyes as he spoke her name and something like ecstasy passed over her face, there and gone in the blink of an eye.

"I can't. I'm not strong enough." Her eyes opened though she kept them downcast, unable or unwilling to meet his stare.

His brows drew together, but he waited for her to continue.

"I'm betrothed," she whispered.

He nodded, but it went unseen.

"I must marry Lord Baxter for my family, for myself. I have to save them." She spoke as though convincing herself, her hands clenched into fists atop her skirt. "I thought I could do it. I thought I was strong enough, but that was before. It was so much easier to say yes when I thought you were only a dream. How can I go through with this when you stand before me as real as the sun and as perfect as the dawn?"

He rose and took a tentative step forward, bolstered when she didn't flinch or move away. Before he could think better of it, he rushed to her, dropping to his knees and taking her in his arms. She didn't fight him this time, flinging her arms around his middle as she pressed her face to his shoulder. She trembled in his grasp and he pulled her closer, wishing he could lend her strength through physical touch alone.

"Oh, Daric," she cried, her voice muffled in the fabric of his jacket. Realizing it, she pulled back enough to see his face. "I feel as though I am drowning. I see you and I know you are my savior, but I fear the only way to keep my family afloat is to let myself be pulled under."

He brought his hands up to cup her face, his thumbs gently brushing away the trails of tears. Though he could barely feel her through the numbing cold, he marveled at being in her proximity. He would swear the sunlight chose that moment to peek through the clouds. When her words finally breached the wall of his blissful ignorance, he became extremely aware of the fragility of their moment together. The damp cold soaked through his pants, reminding him that reality was all around them. No longer could they hide from the world in their enchanted cottage.

"I meant what I said, Alaine." He stared into her eyes, willing her to see the truth reflected in his own. "I needed to find you—to see that you are safe—and I have done that. Of course, I hoped that we could be something more, that we could continue what was started in that little cottage without the shadow of the curse above our heads. But I could not in good conscience ask you to put aside the well-being of yourself or your family to be with me. If marrying this man—" The words caught in his throat and he struggled against the emotion that choked him. "If marrying this man to save your family is what you want, I will respect your wishes. Tell me that this choice will make you happy and I will be satisfied."

Her tears began to fall anew and he leaned forward to press his forehead to hers.

He continued in hushed tones so that not even the trees could overhear what was meant for her ears alone. "No matter what you decide, I want you to know that you are loved."

She sobbed and it broke his heart, but he needed to get the words out before he lost his nerve.

"You are loved and cherished and respected, and you are worthy of it a thousand times over. Your mind is beautiful. Your soul is beautiful. And the world is infinitely better with you in it. Against time and distance, we found each other. I am grateful for the time we had together, however brief it may have been. I wish you peace and happiness in whatever path you walk.

Know that there is nothing that you could do to make me stop loving you."

He let his tears run freely, their combined despair salting the ground between their knees. Far above their heads, a bird cawed, its shrill call echoing like the peal of a bell, calling them back to reality. As though they'd reached some unspoken agreement, they struggled to their feet, both looking worse for the wear.

"Let's get you back home and warm," he said, turning to leave those accursed woods.

He'd barely turned his back to her, then he felt her hand at his elbow, pulling him back.

"If the choice were mine, it would be you." Her voice was feather soft, but he still caught the words.

He tried and failed to put a smile on his face, nodding solemnly. "I know."

CHAPTER 36

Alaine

On their walk back from the forest, Daric recounted his recent encounter with the witch. Alaine's head spun from the knowledge that the witch had supposedly had good intentions from the start. She certainly wasn't as quick to forgive as Daric seemed to be, but she supposed the witch must have been quite convincing to smooth over all his years of trauma.

She and Daric parted ways before her family home came into view. Leaving him went against every instinct she possessed, but she knew introducing him to her family would be more trouble than it was worth. Besides, she didn't need anything to hinder her marriage to Baxter, not when she was so close to freeing her family from this mess. It didn't stop her from turning to look back at him until he disappeared amidst the rolling, grassy hills.

When she arrived at her family's doorstep, Alaine felt like she'd left a part of herself behind in the woods. She looked back once more to where woods had beckoned her all those months ago. Though she could no longer see him, she raised her hand in farewell to Daric, to freedom, to the little girl who'd dared to hope for more and the woman she could have been.

Alaine turned back to the door, taking in the chipped green paint and crumbling façade. Never before had she noticed these minor imperfections. She was surprised they passed her mother's scrutiny, but then it had always been only Alaine who failed to live up to her mother's expectations.

There were tears in her eyes as she opened the door, but she refused to let them fall. She had pitied herself enough. It was time she accepted her responsibilities.

No sooner had she crossed the threshold than her mother pounced, bombarding her with questions about her whereabouts and demanding answers about her state of dress.

Alaine waited for her mother to quiet long enough for her to respond and then spoke clearly and calmly. "I am a grown woman. I am old enough to wed and old enough to make my own decisions. I was feeling overwhelmed and went out for some fresh air. That is all you need to know." Her mother opened her mouth to speak, but Alaine cut her off with a raised hand. "Before you spit any other nonsense, let me remind you that I am marrying a man I hate with every fiber of my being to save this family from financial ruin. The least I deserve is some time to myself before I'm sold off like some breeding mare."

Turning her back to her mother, who stood open-mouthed and wide-eyed, Alaine climbed the stairs to her bed-chamber, ducking her head to hide the slight upturn of her lips.

When she reached her room, she wasn't at all shocked to see the witch—Eudora, Daric had called her—waiting for her within. Alaine hastily stepped inside, closing the door behind her before anyone else could see her visitor. Eyeing Eudora from across the room, she crossed her arms and leaned back against the door. She couldn't be sure that her mother wouldn't follow her up the stairs and barge in on them.

"What do you want?" Alaine had hoped to have more bite in her voice, but the words came out tired.

Eudora looked her up and down, likely noting her disheveled appearance. "You've seen Prince Daric then, I trust?"

Alaine noted the slight changes to the witch's face, just as Daric had described. She *had* changed, though whether for good or bad remained to be seen. "I have," she replied, unwilling to provide too many details. "What business is it of yours?"

"Alaine—"

"Ms. Martan," Alaine corrected stiffly. Perhaps it was petty, but she found she didn't care.

Eudora pressed her lips together and exhaled through her nose. "Ms. Martan, you have to know that I desire only to see you and His Highness reunited."

"Oh, really?" Alaine struggled to keep her voice low, unsure if the room had been spelled. "You keep referring to him as *Prince* Daric and *His Highness* and yet, *you* are the reason he no longer bears that title. You cursed him to centuries of solitude and then cursed me as well. Though you claim to want us together, you tore us apart the very moment I professed my love for him. How am I to believe your good intentions now?"

"You're right to be angry. I underestimated the power of the magic I used to grant his wish, but I fought against it when I could. I gave him the cottage to care for him when no other could. It was I who returned your beauty to you that night we visited. I brought the man you love across the kingdom—nearly to your doorstep—so that you could fulfill his wish and live happily ever after. What more can I do?"

"Nothing!" Alaine had heard enough. All her life she'd had constant interference from her parents, the townspeople, and now this witch. "I am to marry Lord Baxter at the first snowfall." The more she said it, the easier it became, her mouth growing used to the bitter taste on her tongue. "My family needs me and I will do as they ask."

"Alaine—" Eudora reached for her, but Alaine stepped out of reach.

"I think you've done enough. Please go." She motioned toward the door though she was fairly certain the witch hadn't used it when she arrived.

"Daric's wish is not the only one that called to me, you know. I answered yours as well that day in the woods."

"What wish?" Alaine wracked her brain, but couldn't remember having wished for anything. She was usually so careful not to cast out her hopes.

"As I recall, you wished for another way out of this."

Alaine waited for more, but the witch only tilted her head and looked at her expectantly. "Well?" she hissed. "Another way out of what?"

Eudora smiled and while there was no malice to it, Alaine saw a hint of the crafty, scheming woman she'd been before. "A way out of whatever you like. That's the beauty in magic after all. You'll find the true miracle lies not in what is said, but what remains unspoken."

With those cryptic words, the witch disappeared, leaving Alaine alone to ponder the power of a wish and the fate of her family.

CHAPTER 37

Daric

Daric watched Alaine walk away, certain it was the last time he would ever see her. Though he trembled from head to foot, he no longer felt the bite of the winter wind through his dampened clothes. The sun had nearly dipped below the horizon by the time he shook himself free from his numb stupor.

In truth, he didn't know what to do with himself. He had no plan. He'd been following a star and it had winked out of existence, leaving him adrift in a world about which he knew nothing. Enough had changed in the time he'd been cursed that he barely recognized the land he was meant to rule.

He wondered if he had any living relatives, if they knew of him, or if he'd been erased from his legacy as surely as he had the history books.

Since no coin weighed down his pockets, he had few options open to him. He turned his feet toward Maribonne, hoping to find a barn to spend the night until he could sort himself out. There was always physical work to be done. He could find employment as a laborer, just not here. He planned to get far from Maribonne before he could do something reckless like murdering Alaine's betrothed.

The sudden bloodlust came as a shock to him. He'd never been a violent man, but something about Alaine marrying that scum made him see red. If she wasn't so dead set on helping her family, he'd break apart the wedding himself.

He'd barely covered half the distance to the town when he felt a familiar presence at his side. He didn't need to look to know that Eudora had joined him. It felt odd to be comforted by her presence after dreading it for so long. When he glanced sidelong, he found her already watching him, seeming to gauge his intentions as he stalked toward the town.

"You may rest easy, Eudora. I've no plans to kill any lords this evening."

She blew out a breath as though relieved, but he got the feeling she already knew he wouldn't come between Alaine and her future husband. Though the thought made him sick, he respected Alaine enough to make her own choices, as poor as they were. He could only do so much to dissuade her and, as he'd said, he had nothing of value to offer.

"I've booked you a room for this evening at the inn in town," she said.

"I don't need your pity—"

"Then consider it reparations for the hurt I've caused you."

They stopped and he faced her, taken aback by how young and vulnerable she appeared in the moonlight. Aside from her brief stint as a man, Daric had only seen her in this form, the one he'd come to know as the maiden since the curse had been broken. It was possible the other incarnation had come from the being that possessed her. There would be no tears shed by him if he never saw that old crone again though.

He rolled his eyes but nodded in begrudging acquiescence. "Fine. Lead on."

The so-called inn turned out to be little more than an alehouse with a spare room on the second floor, but Daric was grateful for the warm place to rest. His eyelids had grown heavy, his heart even heavier as they trekked across the barren fields. Though he wanted nothing more than to fall into bed, the scent of roasted meat and sour ale sent his stomach rumbling immediately upon entering the inn. Eudora gave him a knowing look as though she'd somehow heard his hunger over the roaring of the busy tavern.

"Let me buy you dinner." He opened his mouth to refuse, but she cut him off before he had the chance. "It is the least I can do. Please do not starve for pride's sake."

"At least join me, then. I don't think I'm in the right headspace to dine alone right now." He wasn't ashamed to admit he needed a friend. Though it was strange for Eudora to fill that role, he had no one else.

She must have seen something in his expression, or maybe she felt the absence of companionship just as sharply, but they found a table along the wall and signaled the barkeep over to take their order.

Daric finally regained feeling in his fingers as two sweating tankards of ale were placed before them. His feet were another issue entirely in his soaking wet boots and he wished they'd gotten a seat closer to the fire. Glancing around for another table, his eyes widened at the crowd he'd somehow ignored till then. He'd known the tavern was loud, but his mind had disconnected from what was happening around him, solely focused on the acquisition of food and warmth.

Every other table in the inn was occupied. People even lingered between tables, waiting for a seat to open up.

All at once, the room became too small and too warm. Bodies pressed in on them from three sides, trapping him in place against the wall and cutting off his air. Beneath the table, his leg bounced in an effort to dispel the nervous energy swelling inside him. Sweat beaded at his temples as his heart rate rose and he became increasingly aware of the way the collar of his shirt rubbed his neck.

Daric closed his eyes and tipped his head against the cool stone wall, fighting to take deep breaths to counter the rising panic.

Too many people.

Too many people.

Too many—

Cool, steady hands brushed his, and delicate tendrils of ice swept over him, calming rather than chilling.

"Big breath in, Daric."

Eudora's voice drowned out the clamor around him. He inhaled deeply, the scent of pine and ozone replacing the stale odor of the inn as she worked her magic.

"And exhale."

Air escaped him in a near-silent *whoosh*. She repeated the directions several times in her hypnotic voice before he felt the tension in his body begin to ease. He kept his eyes closed, refusing to let his vision sabotage his slight progress. Despite Eudora's efforts, his anxiety still lingered, though it had waned significantly with her intervention. He reached blindly for one of her hands, clasping it and giving a gentle squeeze that he hoped conveyed his thanks.

She continued murmuring encouragement and sending cooling magic towards him until his focus was seized by a loud, boisterous laugh from his left.

Before he could think better of it, he opened his eyes and located the source in the crowd. He had no difficulty picking out the offender as his voice continued to carry over the din.

The man stood at a table near the center of the room, one leg propped up on the chair of a companion that he jovially slapped on the back. He seemed well-built, lean, but muscular and taller than most in the room, Daric excluded. Dark hair was slicked back from a face that may as well have been chiseled from stone for all its lack of imperfections. Though his clothing spoke of wealth, his mannerisms suggested he was richer in coin than morality. Even as Daric watched, the man ostentatiously pinched the backside of a passing woman, while bragging of his upcoming nuptials.

It made Daric sick that someone like that would enter into the sanctity of marriage so frivolously.

Eudora gasped when she finally found the object of Daric's focus. The sound drew Daric's gaze from the spectacle for only a moment, but it was long enough to see the recognition flicker over her face. Though she tamped it down quickly, Daric latched onto the knowledge that somehow she knew this man.

He considered where they were, in Alaine's hometown, and pieces of the puzzle clicked into place.

"*That* is Alaine's future husband?" he growled.

Eudora's grip on his hand tightened as his teeth ground together. It took everything in him to keep from jumping out of his seat and confronting the man. If he'd had the security of employment and a place to stay, Daric would be more willing to risk the conflict. As it was, judging by the reactions from the people around him, Alaine's betrothed appeared to be well-regarded among the townsfolk—the men, at least. Daric would need to stay in their favor for as long as he planned to remain.

"Lord Henrik Baxter," muttered Eudora with disdain. "His father owns nearly half the town, but the son acts like he owns it all, the people included. And yes, he *is* Alaine's future husband. I know you don't want to hear this, but I'm not sure she could do worse. I suppose she only needs him for the one thing he's good for."

Daric glanced at her quizzically, hoping she didn't mean what he thought.

"Money." She said it like it was obvious and Daric hoped his face didn't betray his thoughts.

He pulled his hand from hers in case the physical connection somehow allowed her access to his mind. He'd seen crazier things, after all.

"Right," he said, turning his focus back to the spectacle in the middle of the room.

Baxter didn't notice their curious stares among all the others, clearly enjoying being the center of attention. He called for a round of drinks for the room, which resulted in cheers from everyone but the barmaids. As they scrambled to fill tankards, Baxter climbed on a table, raising his drink above his head and almost colliding with the large wrought-iron chandelier suspended from the ceiling. He stomped his boots on the table until the roar of the crowd became a low rumble.

"Ladies," Baxter angled his tankard toward the few women around him, sloshing ale on those below him in the process. "I regret to inform you that I will soon be a married man." A couple of girls shrieked in protest and Baxter pressed his free hand to his heart, a pained expression on his face. "It is unfortunate news indeed that duty has staked its claim on me, but fear not, for I am still a free man for this night at least." Chuckles followed this statement and Baxter felt sorry for the poor wives of these fellows. It was no wonder Alaine held such misguided ideas about love and marriage. "My good fellows, I must also let you know that my bride shall be none other than the beauty, Alaine."

Hoots and hollers abounded and Daric nearly roared at the barmaid that attempted to top off his drink. Eudora pierced him with a look that had him uttering a hasty apology at her retreating form. He felt himself falling back into old habits that reminded him of darker times. Once again, he was alone and tired. So damned tired. The leash on his emotions had frayed, nearly undone by the cruel words spilling from the cock that crowed above them all.

Had he his crown—his title—he would put an end to it all. It wasn't lost on him that he'd given up his kingdom for a love that couldn't exist without it. He turned an assessing glance on Eudora, but she was already shaking her head, likely guessing at the direction of his thoughts.

"I'd like you all to join me in a toast." Around them, cups rose in salute as Baxter prattled on about his perfect life. Daric didn't think he'd ever resented someone more. "To playing the game and winning the prize." Baxter upended his drink, gulping down the last of its contents.

A chorus of *here, here* and *cheers* were accompanied by the clinking of glasses.

Daric's rage became a living thing inside his chest, begging for relief, for action, for anything to douse the flames that burned within him.

Someone placed a steaming bowl of stew on the table before him and another in front of Eudora. He stared at the hearty meal, knowing his body needed it, but unwilling to put forth any more effort into living. It hit him then that without the curse holding him hostage, he could end it. He could just give up, stop trying.

"Don't even think about it." Eudora's sharp whisper startled him out of his trance.

"Stop doing that."

"Then stop wearing your heart on your sleeve. I think your rain cloud may be invading my space and I am not here to mope and feel sorry for myself."

"And why are you here?" He didn't know. He appreciated her help, but beyond her desire to right a wrong, he couldn't fathom why she would stick around. It certainly wasn't because of his charming personality.

"Because," she said, drawing out the last syllable, "unlike you, *I* haven't given up yet. Until Alaine exchanges vows with that sorry excuse for a man, she is not married. That means there is still hope. There is still a chance that this marriage will not happen. It is up to us to ensure that it doesn't happen."

"But why?"

"Because I worked too damn hard finding your perfect match to have this wish slip through my fingers at the last second."

His perfect match. That she was.

Running his hands through his unbound hair, Daric exhaled a long breath. His urge to kill Baxter had ebbed, though he wouldn't turn down the opportunity if it presented itself. Eudora was right. He'd accepted Alaine's marriage as easily as she had. He'd given up on them because she believed there was no other way to save her family, but Daric knew that what seemed impossible often wasn't.

"So, what can we do?" he asked.

Eudora's answering smile was all teeth.

CHAPTER 38

Alaine

A laine woke two days later to an overwhelming sense of dread. Bolting upright in her bed, she scanned the room for any sign of intruders but found nothing to warrant her spike of anxiety. For days, she'd been plagued by fits of unease. Recurring nightmares meant she hadn't gotten a full night's rest since waking in her family home. Her thoughts continued to volley between her impending marriage and an unreasonable fear that she had never freed herself from the curse.

"Everything's fine. You're free and you're saving your family." Alaine repeated the mantra she'd been echoing when the stress became too much, but the words rang hollow. She didn't feel free. In fact, she felt more caged now than she ever had in the cottage.

Sighing, she stretched back out on the bed, pulling her blanket up to her chin in the hope that it would provide some measure of comfort. Her eyelids quickly grew heavy as sleep beckoned once again. She'd nearly given in to the dark embrace when her eyes flew open and flicked to the window, latching onto the faint glow that slipped past the curtains.

She'd grown accustomed to the warm rays of the sun creeping in to wake her at the cottage, but here the sun didn't reach her window until afternoon. It certainly didn't account for the cool radiance that illuminated her bed chamber.

The floorboards creaked as she slipped from her bed, her toes curling against the unwelcome cold. Her feet were leaden as she closed the distance to the window, but her body tensed as though readying for action. It took a moment for her mind to catch up to the wakefulness of her body, but when it did, the pieces of the puzzle slid into place. Throwing aside the curtains, she pressed her face to the glass, her look of horror etching in the frost that coated it as she watched the glittering snowflakes fall to the ground.

Snow had come to Maribonne.

It would be beautiful on any other day, but today it was a chilling reminder of what awaited. At last and all too soon, the day of her wedding had arrived.

Her skin grew cold where it pressed against the glass, but she remained staring out her window as the tiny flakes became a fine dusting that coated every surface.

Her attention snagged on a single black speck floating in the sea of white. She watched as it grew larger and larger until the lone raven perched on one of the branches outside her window. It was near enough that if she opened the window, she could stroke a finger along its oil-slick feathers.

They stared at one another and the raven cocked its head to one side. Feeling only slightly foolish, Alaine waved to the bird. It gave her another little twitch of its head in response and hopped in place to turn away from her. When the bird spread its wings, preparing for flight, it gave one final look over its shoulder as if inviting her along. Alaine shook her head and a sudden pang of longing made her chest ache as the bird soared into the sky without another glance for her.

The house was quiet. She must have been the first to wake, for surely her mother would have swept in to dress her already if she knew. Alaine collapsed against the windowsill, everything in her screaming to take her chances and run, her family be damned. She wondered if she could find Daric again. Wondered if he'd gone far away from here the first chance he'd gotten.

Could they piece together a life from the feelings between them? How would her family survive in her absence?

If only they cared enough about her to give up their life of status. Daric was starting over. They could all start over. If Eudora was truly on their side, she could lead them to the cottage. It might not possess the same enchantment, but they could get on just fine with a roof overhead and a forest to hunt and forage. They'd be stronger together, especially with love guiding them instead of fear.

Alaine almost convinced herself, optimism eating away at her anxiety. Her mother would never agree, her stubborn pride like an iron wall. But her father, perhaps he could be persuaded to her side.

She'd have to try.

Walking the aisle to Baxter would be that much harder if she didn't exhaust every possible option first.

As the sounds of the stirring household wafted through the crack beneath her door, Alaine took up a brush, slipped off her bonnet, and began untangling her tresses.

Her mother arrived several moments later in a flurry of ruffles and excitement. She'd had her finest gown embellished with lace and pearls for the occasion. A fur stole completed her winter wedding ensemble. She had clearly dressed in a hurry, her hair still hanging loose around her shoulders in a way that suddenly reminded Alaine how young her mother was.

Alaine had often suspected that her parents' marriage had not been a love match. Though they'd fallen into a sort of mutual appreciation and camaraderie, they had likely been matched for social gain. She knew her mother resented being matched with a craftsman. Alaine's paternal grandfather had been one of the most affluent artisans in the province, but if she had to guess, her mother probably hoped to wed someone like Baxter—perhaps even the senior Lord Baxter. It didn't change how Alaine felt about the marriage, but it helped paint her mother in a new light.

Her mother chittered enthusiastically, lost to the task of readying her only daughter for her wedding day, wholly ignorant to the tension that had existed between them since her fitting.

In no time, Alaine was pinned, lacquered, dusted with powder, and stuffed into her wedding dress, now altered to fit snug to her curves. When she caught a glimpse of herself in the mirror, she had a flashback to her first day under the curse's power. For the second time in her life, a stranger stared back at her. Only this time, there was no sense of relief, no anticipation of the unknown. There was only this body she'd been forced to inhabit, dancing to the strings of her puppet master, forever bending to the whims of others.

She was going to be sick.

"I need some air." It was the best excuse she could muster as her stomach heaved.

"We are expected at the Town Hall at noon!" exclaimed her mother, her hands on her hips.

"I'll only be a moment." That was a lie, but there were still several hours until noon. She pushed past her mother, nearly falling in her haste to slip on her boots. Somehow she maintained enough sense to grab her fur-lined cloak on her way out the door.

After several deep breaths of crisp, cool air, her nausea ebbed. Fearing it may return if she stepped back inside, she let her feet carry her away. She was grateful she'd insisted on boots as her feet sank into the fresh snow. It crunched beneath her feet, a steady rhythm to match the ticking of the clock that chased her, her freedom drawing to an end.

She stopped at the fork in the road, once again coming to a crossroads in her life. Glancing east, she saw the tips of the forest trees. She didn't think she would ever be able to step foot in those woods again without thinking of Daric and the too-brief time they'd shared.

The silence was deafening, the world holding its breath as she struggled to decide her course.

Growing up, the first snow had always felt like magic, a blanket of glitter to decorate the dead landscape of winter. Today, it felt like a beautiful shroud being pulled over her head, like the end of joy, of youth, of *life*. How strange it felt to be mourning what she lost when those around her celebrated. It was perhaps the most out of place she'd ever felt in her hometown.

Alaine lifted her hand in silent farewell, then turned her back to the forest and trudged toward the town. With any luck, the other townspeople would not be out and about in this weather. Marrying Baxter wouldn't mean she had to leave town, but she desired closure on this aspect of her life and she didn't need an audience for the task.

As the town grew closer, she realized she had avoided it completely since her return from the forest. Aside from her brief time in the woods with Daric, she'd been confined to her parents' home. Visiting now felt like returning to the scene of a crime. She remembered the burning stares, the harsh words, the possessive touches. What she struggled to remember were the good moments, for surely there had been positive memories created here too. Alaine delved deep within but was unable to recall anything other than pain and disappointment.

She thought if she was the main character in one of her novels, she might just burn it all to the ground. However, though she resented the people of Maribonne, she couldn't bring herself to cause them harm. Just like she couldn't stand to be the cause of her family's suffering.

As she walked, the time-worn footpath became a wide avenue. The houses grew taller and closer together, interspersed with businesses of all manners, all closed to the inclement weather. As suspected, there were very few others milling about the town. Two small children laughed and played in the freshly fallen snow, their guardian observing from beneath a nearby overhang. A man rushed past her so quickly she didn't get a look at his face before he stomped away. A couple stepped out from the Magistrate's office, whispering to one another as they huddled close together.

No, not a couple.

Daric and Eudora.

The witch's fiery red hair stood out in stark contrast to the white-washed world around them. Alaine stood too far away to hear their words or read the expressions on their faces, but when Daric leaned in close, they looked for all the world like a young couple in love. Her heart seized at the sight. Though she no longer had any claim to him, in fact, she hoped that he would find happiness after everything, it caused her physical pain to see him with another. Never mind that it was the very witch who claimed to be helping them.

Alaine's blood boiled. She swore she saw snowflakes turn to steam as they touched her skin. Half of her wanted to sink back into the shadows, but the other half—the half currently in control—demanded she march over and confront them.

Daric saw her coming before she'd taken two steps toward them. His eyes widened at her approach, causing Eudora to whip her head towards Alaine as well. Their faces quickly turned guarded as she neared them and she donned a mask of cool apathy in response.

"Fancy seeing you here together," she said looking pointedly between the pair, "and on my wedding day, no less."

Daric winced at the mention of her upcoming nuptials and Alaine felt her teeth clench in irritation. How dare he parade around *her* town with another woman and have the nerve to react to her impending coupling. Clearly, he'd moved on just fine in a matter of days.

"Alaine," Daric seemed at a loss for words, his eyes roving over her from head to toe. "You look beautiful."

She gave him a flat stare in return. "Yes, I know." She couldn't stop the fire that spewed from her mouth. Of all the things to say, those three words held the least meaning to her. All her life she'd been told the same thing over and over again—*you are beautiful*—and look where it had gotten her. "You two look cozy."

"What is that supposed to mean?" asked Eudora, a crease forming between her brows.

Alaine crossed her arms, cocking her hip to the side as raised a single brow in question. "Don't insult me. You think I don't see what's going on here?"

Daric shared an exasperated look with Eudora and ran his hands through his hair. "It's not like that, Alaine. I know you're hurting right now, but we don't deserve to be the focus of your anger."

"Oh, really? She served no part in this? Is that what you're telling me?" Alaine scoffed. "What are you even doing here? I thought you'd be long gone by now."

"Alaine—Ms. Martan," Eudora corrected herself at Alaine's icy stare, "we are here to help. We'll figure out a way to get you out of this."

"There is no way out!" Alaine cried, choking back a sob that verged on hysteria. She looked at Daric, grim determination painting his features. "Don't you see? I wondered how life could be so perfect under a supposed curse, but I was wrong. *This* is the curse." Her arms flailed about in an effort to fully encompass everything wrong with her life. "And there's no undoing it. Not for lack of trying."

Alaine felt her nausea return as Daric shared another glance with Eudora, who nodded once, then stepped away to afford them some measure of privacy.

Daric inched closer to her, hand outstretched as if to clasp hers. Alaine pulled away, regretting the action immediately as a flash of hurt crossed his face.

"Someone might see," she murmured by way of explanation.

He blew out a breath, the air condensing into a puff of smoke between them. "I saw him, the man you are to marry, and I promise I will do all in my power to make sure you never wed the likes of him. He is a disease among men—one that should be eradicated—not someone to be revered."

All this she knew, but it didn't change the fact that she had no other options.

He must have read the surrender on her face. "I may not have much to give, but you need only ask it of me and it is yours. You told me that you would choose me if you could. Alaine, I choose you. I will always choose you. I love you and, if you'll have me, I will marry you. You are my queen, the one I yearned for—*skies*, the one I cursed myself for. We shall rule over nothing but our own lives and that will be enough. *You* are enough. Don't give up on us."

Alaine had never longed for love, at least not aloud. She knew better than to wish for the secret desire that lingered in the dark recesses of her heart, but Daric's words sparked a flame of hope in her chest.

"I apologize for how I spoke." She caught Eudora's eye as she cautiously rejoined their space. "I'm just so scared." A laugh bubbled out of her, but it morphed into a sob that wracked her body. She pressed a fist to her chest, forcing her emotions back into the tiny box she kept within.

"I don't think I actually believed this day would come. It's like a nightmare. I keep pinching myself, thinking I'll wake up back at the cottage in our own little world." Her mouth pulled up on one side, the closest thing to a smile she could manage. She hugged her arms around herself and blinked up at the sky, expelling a large breath as she tried to keep the tears at bay.

Gentle, but sure arms wrapped around her in a comforting embrace and she looked down to find Eudora. Alaine searched her face, finding no trace of judgment. A few paces away, Daric clenched and unclenched his hands, no doubt battling his own desire to pull her to him.

Alaine considered herself lucky to have known both of them. For whatever direction life pulled her, she was glad to have two people who saw her true self and didn't shy away from her flaws. She rolled her eyes but waved for Daric to join them. Within moments, Eudora and Alaine were engulfed in his strong arms.

Though the inauspicious snow continued to fall around them, Alaine reveled in how it felt to love and be loved in return.

CHAPTER 39

Daric

Tears streaked Alaine's painted face when they finally pulled apart. Though he'd meant it when he told her she looked beautiful, he could see the cracks in her armor, the cosmetics doing little to hide the haunted look in her eyes. And to think, it was all for that bastard, Baxter. Daric's teeth ground together just thinking about him. At that moment, he'd do anything to take down her hair and wash her face—to see the real Alaine beneath the mask.

Alaine apologized again to Eudora, who waved her off with the kind of nonchalance one only achieved after centuries alive.

"There is always hope," said Eudora with more certainty than he possessed. "We are trying."

Though she nodded in understanding, Daric watched Alaine's walls rebuild brick by brick as she fortified her defenses.

She was so strong and yet, he hated that she needed to be. Hated that he couldn't solve every problem and thwart every enemy that came her way. He wanted nothing more than to take her far away, but they'd need a miracle to see her and her family freed from their fates. She looked at him with a hopeless mix of sorrow and longing, but he knew she hadn't changed her mind. She would go through with the marriage if that's what it took to save her family.

"If it doesn't—" Daric fought to get the words out, his tongue thick and mouth dry. "If you have to go through with it—" He wouldn't speak it into reality. Words held more power than people realized. "What I mean is, I'll wait for you. Always. If you decide it isn't the life you want, I'll be there in a heartbeat. Ten, twenty, fifty years from now, it doesn't matter. If I remember correctly, I think I still owe him a beating on your behalf." His lips quirked up in a smile that she returned with tears in her eyes.

Alaine nodded, solemn determination stiffening her spine. She turned to leave and his hand instinctively reached out to pull her back. He resisted the urge to touch her, knowing she feared repercussions if they were seen, but she paused as though sensing his intentions.

"Thank you, Daric."

The words drifted to him in the icy wind, chilling him to the core. To his ears, it sounded like goodbye. He wished he had made a point to memorize the lines of her face in case he never saw her again, but she didn't look back. Not this time.

Days ago, he'd been resigned to a life without her, but today there was hope and he intended to help it bloom.

He threw a cursory glance to where Eudora stood nearby. "We have work to do."

CHAPTER 40

Alaine

A laine rushed back to her parents' home as quickly as she could manage in the deepening snow, weighed down by dark thoughts and a heavy heart.

When she arrived, there was a black carriage waiting out front. A large gold B adorned the door, letting her know exactly who had sent it. At least, she hoped that Baxter had sent it for her family and wasn't presently waiting inside. She had not mentally prepared herself to see her betrothed just yet.

The horse whinnied as she tiptoed toward the door. She hushed the creature with soft murmurs and placating gestures. Alaine hadn't spent much time around horses and this one looked as terrifying to her as its master.

Muffled voices drifted through the crack beneath the door and she pressed her ear to the wood in an attempt to distinguish who waited on the other side. The shrill chatter indicated her mother remained within, but the responding voice was too low to make out and she couldn't be sure there was only one male within. That alone made her reconsider entering through the front. The rear door offered little more in the way of secrecy and she found herself at an impasse.

She retreated a step and the horse nickered, forcing her to sidestep around to the back of the carriage. Luckily, her parents had the shutters closed against the bitter cold. She'd hate to be discovered sneaking around outside.

Unwilling to return to the village, Alaine found herself out of options. She decided to take her chances around back rather than face her family and potentially Baxter. Trudging through the snow was becoming increasingly more difficult as the snow drifts deepened toward the back of the house. She came up short when she spotted the large sycamore whose bare branches reached right up to her bedroom window.

It had been years since Alaine had climbed a tree, even longer since she'd climbed this particular tree. In her youth, she'd often scaled its branches when sneaking in or out, but that practice had stopped when she'd fallen and torn one of her mother's favorite dresses. Her mother had been so upset about the dress that Alaine hid her limp from the resulting injury for weeks until it healed. She hadn't been willing to attempt the climb again since.

Taking stock of the snow-covered boughs and wondering how her worn leather boots and gown would fare, insecurity flared to life in her belly. She tamped down on the fluttering nerves and blew out through her mouth, resolved to avoid her future husband for as long as possible.

She stepped up to the thick trunk, bracing one foot on the sill of the lower window as she hoisted herself up, leaning against the trunk until she could wrap her arms around the lowest lying branch. Her feet scrambled for purchase against the slick bark as she fought to raise her body bit by bit. Eventually, she found a rhythm and climbed until she reached her room on the second floor.

Her frozen fingers struggled to pry open the window, but with the help of some careful maneuvering, she finally broke into her room.

The door was closed and though very little of the household heat had reached it, it felt like a sauna after so much time in the storm.

Alaine peeled off her soaking wet gloves, setting them on the table beside her mirror, and nearly gasped when she caught a glimpse of her reflection. What little cosmetics remained dribbled down her cheeks and jaw, streaks of white, black, and pink tracing the skin like tears. Her hair was a limp mess atop her head. The dress her mother had so lovingly selected lay torn and dirty over her frame.

Before she could think to stop it, a laugh bubbled out of her. It surprised her enough that she clapped a hand over her mouth, listening intently for any approaching footsteps.

When no one came calling, she hurriedly locked the door for good measure. Now that she was inside the house, she could distinctly hear the voices of her mother, her father, and another man, presumably the coachman since she didn't recognize it as Baxter's. The second man spoke with urgency, hoping to lure her parents into the carriage with haste. It seemed her parents refused to leave without her.

That was fine.

With the door firmly locked, Alaine paid no mind to the amount of noise she made as she stripped off her sodden clothes. She missed her wardrobe at the enchanted cottage as she opened up her closet to select another outfit. Her selection was paltry compared to what the cottage had produced, but she did have one dress she deemed appropriate for the occasion.

As the only black garment she possessed, she'd only been permitted to wear it to somber occasions, her grandfather's funeral being the most recent. Her wedding to Baxter was surely a somber occasion and she donned it without hesitation. She sighed as the rich dark wool slid over her bare skin. It was far more comfortable than the other dress had been. And warmer.

She wiped her face clean and brushed out her hair, choosing to leave it unbound as she finally unlocked her door and stepped out to the waiting gazes of her parents.

Their eyes met through the uprights of the banister, all parties falling silent upon her appearance. Her mother's cool gaze assessed her from head to toe, but she wisely kept quiet upon seeing Alaine's steely expression.

The stairs creaked as she descended slowly, but purposefully, the only other sound the nervous pacing of the coachman. Her father gave her a single nod, a hint of a smile crinkling his eyes before they shifted to her mother and stayed there, watching her warily like a snake about to strike. However, despite the stormy expression marring her painted features, her mother remained silent until Alaine's foot lifted from the final step.

As they stood motionless, staring at one another from across the room, Alaine was surprised to note the flicker of hurt that passed over her mother's face. It had never been her intention to cause her parents pain. In fact, until this moment, she'd gone out of her way to obey their wishes—had literally thrown away her chance at the life she desired in order to save them.

Her resentment must have shown on her face for her mother simply sniffed and strode to the door, the coachman following close on her heels.

The door whipped open on a gust of air and snow billowed inside like an unwelcome guest. Beyond, the horse stamped with impatience, tossing his head irritably to urge them along.

Her father stepped up to her side and offered his arm, leaning in close as she looped her arm around his. He made no move toward the door. Alaine's own feet could not be persuaded to initiate the momentum.

"It shames me that I must ask this of you, dear one." He sounded tired, and Alaine wondered how she had failed to notice the change in his voice these past weeks. The gradual deterioration from age and stress was now a pronounced croaking rasp that hurt her to hear, no matter how welcome his words. "Lord Baxter is not the man I would have chosen for you, were it my decision, and I believe you share the sentiment."

Their shared look said everything she could not speak aloud.

"A part of me hoped you would not return this morning," he said boldly.

She was grateful for her father's steady presence at her arm as she rocked from the shock of that statement. "I must admit, I've thought about leaving more often than is proper, but I could never live with myself if I left you to this awful mess."

Her father nodded sagely. "It is just as well, I don't know what we could have done if you'd gone. Your mother—" he sighed, "she wants only what is best for all of us. It's no excuse, but she doesn't know Lord Baxter as you and I do. She sees not the tormentor, but the savior, and thus, your impertinence comes as a bit of a shock to her."

"I understand, but I can't bring myself to forgive her as I stand on the precipice of marriage to that villain." Alaine turned to face her father head-on. They were nearly the same height now as he stooped with age. "I'll not willfully sabotage this wedding, but I want you to know I have—" she stumbled on the word that felt foreign on her tongue, "friends, who are working on a solution to our problem. One that doesn't involve Lord Baxter."

"I see." Her father's expression became contemplative as he focused on something over her shoulder. "It would bring me much joy to see you free of all this."

"Thank you, Father." Alaine felt relieved to have him on her side through this and she leaned on calm strength to help her move.

With a kiss on her cheek, her father finally ushered her out to the awaiting carriage.

CHAPTER 41

Alaine

The difficult journey to town through the storm was made all the more uncomfortable by the thick tension between Alaine and her mother. For half the ride, her mother stewed in silence beside her father, throwing disapproving looks at Alaine, who sat across from them. Either they crossed some invisible threshold, or her mother had reached her limit just as Maribonne appeared in their sights, but as they entered the town proper, she exploded.

"I thought I raised you better than this," her mother seethed. She waved her hands in the direction of Alaine's skirts. "This petty protest cannot go unaddressed. You look as though you are headed to a funeral and *not* about to be wedded to a Lord. What happened to the dress I chose for you?"

Alaine opened her mouth to explain, but she couldn't get a word in before her mother continued her tirade.

"You have been blessed with everything you could ever want. You are beautiful beyond compare. Men line up at our door for permission to court you. We gave you a roof over your head and food to fill your belly without asking you to lift a finger. You have books and clothes and parents who love you. You think you are the first unwilling bride? This is your one duty to your family, for all that we have done for you, and you don't even have the decency to pretend to be grateful for it."

Rant over, her mother crossed her arms and turned her head to the ever-falling snow. Alaine looked beseechingly at her father, who only shrugged with an expression that said *I told you so.*

Alaine knew if she responded in anger, her words would tear apart the fragile threads still connecting them. They were standing on opposite sides of a raging river, but regret would not repair the bridge if she burned it.

"I am sorry you feel that way." Alaine kept her voice neutral, leashing her anger even as it threatened to overwhelm her. "I am more than grateful for all that you and Father have provided me, but you need to understand two things. First and foremost, you don't own me. You may have spawned me, cared for me, and raised me, but I am a grown woman and I belong wholly to myself and no other. Second, I do not owe you a single thing. A child does not incur debt by existing and requiring care. All that I do for you, I do because I love you both and I want to see you happy and well. So, no, Mother, I will not put on a smile and act as though you are doing me a favor by marrying me off to this horrid man. You can sit there and be grateful that I am not cursing you to a winter on the streets, or I can ask them to stop this carriage and you can return home. Either way, I will see that this debt is taken care of by nightfall."

The horse's hooves beat a steady pace, the carriage rattling at every bump of the uneven ground. The wind whistled outside the window, but not a sound escaped from the three inside as they sat in stunned silence.

Even Alaine was shocked by her words that still lingered in the air. She examined them for any hint of regret but found them to be sure of purpose and true to her feelings. Try as she might to hate the witch, she was proud of the version of herself that she found in the forest. Being with Daric had turned her into her true self and that, above all else, was what she would miss if she had to marry Baxter.

Her mother sniffled and Alaine had to resist the urge to roll her eyes as her father offered a comforting embrace. Maybe her mother needed to spend some time cursed.

All too soon, the carriage stopped, the coachman opening the door and unfolding the small steps just as the bells began to peal the time. Alaine counted twelve chimes while her father exited and turned to help her mother down. She waited for him to return for her, but her mother pulled him away, already engaging in conversation with the Lord and Lady Ultrich.

She sighed through her nose and lifted her skirts to descend when a familiar hand opened in front of her.

Baxter appeared to step out of thin air as he materialized beside the carriage, an outstretched hand offered in assistance.

"My dear Alaine." Baxter's smile was vinegar. It left a bad taste in her mouth as she eyed the proffered hand.

Ignoring him completely, she turned as best she could within the confines of the carriage and backed down the steps until her feet firmly touched ground. She felt Baxter's assessing stare even before she turned, inspecting the goods before he followed through with his purchase. It didn't surprise her to find his eyes still dancing over her form when she whirled to face him. Her chin lifted in defiance of his perusal. She made sure to keep her arms tight to her sides, resisting the urge to cover herself, even as the feel of his gaze sent shivers down her spine.

"You look—" His eyes did one final sweep of her body from head to toe. "Lovely."

Alaine cocked an eyebrow at that, certain she looked anything but how he'd expected his bride to appear.

The wind whipped her unbound hair across her face. With her long black gown and billowing cloak a stark contrast to the fluffy, falling snow, she probably appeared more like a haunting specter than a bride.

"And you look—" She paused to give him the same all-over stare. "Cold and wet."

His smile turned brittle and Alaine saw the quick flare of anger before he extinguished it. She had refused to acknowledge the memories of bruises in the shape of his fingers. Now that she stared at them head-on, she feared the man she would face behind closed doors. Not a loving husband, but a vengeful lover.

His expression turned hungry as she took an involuntary step back, provoking the hunter within.

"How did you do it?" He looked perplexed at her questions, so she tried rephrasing. "How did you plant the false debt? How does even the Magistrate believe it is real?"

His eyes lit in understanding and he prowled closer, glancing around to confirm no one was in earshot. "My dear Alaine. I should have known you'd figure me out. It was easy enough to forge the necessary documents. My family's standing makes it such that my word is never questioned."

"Why admit it to me now?" she whispered.

His answering chuckle was anything but merry. "I have nothing to fear. Everyone knows you are trying to get out of this marriage and none of them will take your word over mine."

He was right. Every time she'd inquired to see the paperwork, they'd laughed at her and called her a silly little girl playing with affairs best left to men. Alaine didn't understand how the world had come to be defined by gender. How what lay between her thighs meant that she was fit to do some things and not others. The limitations were baffling to her. For surely, all that should matter was her sharp mind and honest heart.

She nearly screamed at the frustration of it all. But she trusted Daric to do what she couldn't and prayed he and Eudora had more success than she.

"I don't know what you're hoping to gain from this marriage, Henrik. Perhaps you are only hoping to add another prize to your collection, but I promise you will be sorely disappointed."

"It won't matter. You will be mine and no one else's. That will be enough."

He took her arm in a vice-like grip that gave her instant flash-backs, but she resisted the urge to twist out of his grasp. Let her mother see what she was selling her daughter into. She would do her duty as promised.

CHAPTER 42

Daric

A crowd had formed in the square despite the still falling snow, no doubt to bear witness to the spectacle. Though the presence of so many people grated on his nerves, it was his stress for Alaine that held him in place. He spotted her the instant she descended the carriage steps, looking like something out of a dream, like a wild beauty forged deep within the forest. She was magnificent, and that sorry excuse for a man *dared* to lay his hands on her. Daric watched from across the busy street, his vision turning red as he observed the possessive way he touched her. He forced himself to take a deep breath in and out, unclenching his fists from where he held them rigid at his sides.

He felt Eudora's hand on his shoulder, like a tether holding him back from making what would potentially be a stupid mistake.

"He seeks only to possess that which does not wish to be owned," she whispered at his back. "We will see this righted. Remember, she chose you above all others."

The words did little to ease the anger that roiled in his belly, but he felt his shoulders lower as he regained his composure. Eudora spoke the truth. Everything would be settled in time, but he had no patience for the bumbling Magistrate that was the final piece in their plan.

"I'm going over there," he growled.

"Wait. You can't just barge in on them without cause."

"Oh, I have plenty of cause." The look she gave him said she still disapproved, but his skin was crawling with the need to intercede. "If we wait too long, she will be married already. Stay if you must, but join me when all is settled. It is time we put an end to this charade."

Though she still looked skeptical, Eudora nodded her consent, biting her lip as she glanced through the window into the Magistrate's office. The old man sat hunched over a pile of documents at his desk, perusing each at a snail's pace, his wire frame spectacles threatening to topple from his pointed nose at any moment.

Daric shook his head ruefully and began to wind his way through the throng, focusing on his breathing as bodies pressed against him from all sides. His temper strained against his hold as he strode across the square, his gaze zeroing in on the hand pressed to Alaine's lower back. He assumed the older couple she'd arrived with were her parents. They stood off to one side, blissfully ignorant of their daughter's torment. Though he had strong words for them as well, he couldn't be bothered to spare them a glance as he passed, not as Baxter and Alaine disappeared inside the hall.

He hurried his steps to catch up and found the way blocked by two liveried men. As one, they moved to stand between him and the door, touching their hands to their belted swords, but not drawing them.

"I am here for the wedding," Daric said through gritted teeth. He didn't wish to make a scene and draw unwanted attention.

The man on the right looked him up and down, likely noting the way that Daric was dressed, which was to say not at all appropriate to attend an event of such caliber. "Are you, now?" The man's voice was thick with sarcasm.

Though Daric's gut told him to silence the man and push through, his good sense won out and he opted for words over weapons. He'd learned that words, when wielded by the right person, could be just as dangerous as a blade.

"I have traveled far to attend this wedding. I am a guest."

"Not any guest that I know," said the man on the left. His skin was pink from the cold, his upturned nose completing the swine-like appearance. "Anyway, guests aren't being allowed in yet. You'll have to wait with everyone else and be checked against the guest list."

"I am an honored guest of the bride and you would do well to let me pass."

Daric felt a presence at his back and braced for the imminent attack, willing to go down swinging if it meant he'd done all he could to reach Alaine. Eudora would look out for her if he failed.

"He is with us, Gregory."

The soft, yet steady voice that came from behind him was not that of another guard, but Alaine's father. Daric schooled his features into neutrality in an attempt to hide his shock as the guards looked between Alaine's father and himself.

"You know this man?" The first man directed his question to her father but raised his eyebrows at Daric.

"Indeed. He is very dear to my daughter. She would be quite distressed if he was barred entrance." Her father's tone brooked no argument as he stopped beside him. Daric risked a glance toward the shorter man, noting hair and eyes the same color as Alaine's.

Daric wondered how much her father knew, or if he only guessed at his connection to Alaine. There didn't appear to be any malicious intent in helping him. Although, he couldn't say the same for his wife. Alaine's mother looked at him like she was sizing up a prize stallion for breeding. Her nose turned up at his travel-worn clothes, but she made no move to reveal her husband's deception, likely playing along until she decided which side better served her purpose.

After a long look passed between them, the guards let them pass, the pig-nosed one holding the door open for them.

"Thank you for your assistance," said Daric as he and Alaine's parents squeezed through the doorway.

He desperately wanted to find Alaine but didn't want to give his savior the wrong impression by rushing off immediately. He kept his pace slow but steady as they entered a large hall with rows upon rows of wooden benches. A center aisle cut through the sea of seats adorned with winter blooms and ribbon. The aisle led to a small, raised dais, illuminated by hundreds of white pillar candles. A large stained glass window threw rainbows throughout the room, dulled but still visible though the storm raged on. The vaulted ceilings echoed every faint sound and Daric lightened his gait to match the hush of the few others present. None of the faces he saw matched the one he sought.

Alaine's father gave him a knowing smile once they were out of earshot of the guards. "You must be the reason my daughter sneaks off to the forest. I am Albair Martan," he said, extending his hand.

"Daric." The man's slight stature belied the strength of his handshake. Taken aback by that show of strength, Daric didn't think to pull away as Alaine's father studied his ring. His *family* ring.

"That's quite the trinket you wear."

Daric smiled and nodded his head in thanks as he casually returned his hand to his side. It would be quite a feat to recognize the signet ring of a monarchy hundreds of years past, but he wouldn't put it past Alaine's cunning-eyed father, who continued to regard him sidelong as they strode shoulder to shoulder down the aisle.

"If you'll excuse me, Mr. Martan. I must find Alaine."

"Of course." Albair bowed slightly at the waist. "She'll be with her intended and the officiant through those doors."

He motioned to a set of doors that Daric hadn't noticed in his initial perusal of the hall. Tucked in the corner beside the dais stood a pair of unremarkable and unmarked doors.

Daric nodded his thanks and set off in the indicated direction, leaving Alaine's parents behind. He'd almost reached the doors when they swung outward of their own accord, revealing two men engaged in conversation; a tall, thin man in ceremonial robes and the man Daric knew to be Lord Baxter. And beyond, in all her dark and wild splendor, waited Alaine.

He knew the moment she saw him, her face transforming from sullen and resigned to bright and exuberant in an instant. She pushed her way between the two men, both looking on with identical expressions of confusion. The distance between them melted away as she sprinted for Daric, leaping up to wrap her arms around his neck. His own arms encircled her swiftly and it felt like coming home. He inhaled the honey lavender scent of her and picked up gentle notes of snow and pine as well.

When her breathing hitched, he pulled her closer, afraid she'd disappear in a cloud of smoke.

Although it was still premature, he could wait no longer. "We did it, Alaine," he whispered. "You're free."

CHAPTER 43

Alaine

T hough she'd seen him only hours before, Alaine had refused to see that moment as anything but another chance
to say goodbye. Seeing him now, and hearing him speak the
words she'd been too afraid to hope for, opened the floodgates
deep inside her.

Sobs wracked her body as her emotions skipped from elation
to relief and everything in between. She pressed her face to
Daric's chest, committing the feel of him to memory in case
something else sought to tear them asunder. His cheek came
to rest against the top of her head and he murmured into her
hair. Though she couldn't distinguish his words over the sound
of her own weeping, his voice was a comforting rumble in her
ears.

Someone cleared their throat nearby, cutting into her and
Daric's too-quick reunion.

Daric's coat, already soaked through by the snow, looked no
worse from her tears when she pulled away.

"What in the skies is going on here?"

She turned and nearly balked at the anger she felt pouring
off Baxter like the heat of a flame. Fury ignited within her in
response and she became vaguely aware of Daric's hands slip-

ping from her back as she stalked forward, the prey becoming the hunter.

The cocky fool did not see it coming when she hauled her arm back and let it swing. Her mother shrieked her name at the same time Daric released a surprised chortle, but no one was more surprised by her punch than Alaine herself.

Her knuckles throbbed as she held them to her chest, but she smiled as color bloomed along Baxter's left cheekbone.

Momentarily shocked into silence, Baxter brushed his fingertips over the injury, wincing even as he worked his jaw open and closed. He remembered himself at the same time Alaine realized what she had done.

She cursed herself for retreating as he advanced one step, then two. Her one punch was nothing compared to his own capabilities for retaliation. Shrinking back, she startled as Daric stepped between her and her approaching foe.

"You'll not lay a hand on her ever again." Her toes curled at the promise of violence in Daric's voice. Never in all their time together had he shown her anything but courtesy. Though she'd come to fear Baxter's displays of power, she found Daric's protectiveness oddly alluring. The difference being that it was fueled by his love for her and would never be directed at her.

Baxter straightened to his full height in acknowledgment of the threat against him. "We are to be married."

"I think if you ask Alaine, you'll find that is no longer the case."

Alaine knew the smirk Daric wore without seeing his face, the sour expression on Baxter's face the exact opposite.

"What is the meaning of this, Alaine?"

Her mother's shrill voice echoed through the hall and Alaine suppressed a groan at the interruption. Tossing a glance over her shoulder, she could see her father attempting to hold back her agitated mother, making placating gestures with his hands and murmuring as Alaine had to Baxter's horse only an hour ago. The sight almost made Alaine laugh, but she bit her tongue to hold in the inappropriate reaction.

Her mother quickly brushed past her father, leaving him trailing in her wake as she stormed down the aisle toward them. Alaine turned to face her head-on, angling her body slightly in front of Daric. Not that she could provide any protection for him, or that he'd need it, but she wanted to be clear on whose side she stood.

"It is as Daric says, Mother. I will not be marrying Lord Baxter today, or any day for that matter." Though the words came out clearly, her hands shook violently. She clasped them behind her to hide her nerves.

Her mother looked at Daric like he was waste in the gutter and Alaine felt her protective instincts rear up. She tensed, preparing to—she didn't know what. She never got the chance to find out as Daric placed a comforting, yet commanding hand over hers, letting her know all was well.

She sighed. "Can you just listen for a moment? Close your mouth and open your mind. Daric's taken care of everything." She turned to look at him, an eyebrow raised in a question. "Right?"

He opened his mouth to speak, but Baxter finally regained his composure enough to intercede.

"Not so fast," he said, pulling her from Daric's hold.

Quick as lighting, Daric broke Baxter's hold, clutching Alaine to his chest as Baxter cradled his arm. "Touch her again and I will end you."

Outrage colored Baxter's face purple as he spluttered. "This marriage has been long in coming. Who are you to dissolve this betrothal? What say do you have on the matter?" He looked around, searching for allies in the small gathering and finding only the confused officiant, who shrugged but offered no further comment. "We don't even know this man. Mr. Martan," Baxter found her father observing it all away from the fray. "Surely, you do not intend to renege on our agreement. What of our deal?"

Alaine's father appeared calm and collected, the complete opposite of her mother who still seethed a few paces away. "It would seem, Lord Baxter, that the terms of the deal may be a moot point now. If we are to believe His Majesty."

CHAPTER 44

Daric

Silence reigned once more as the word settled.

The prick had the nerve to look around as though expecting the monarch to spring out of the woodwork.

How Alaine's father had put the pieces together, Daric didn't know. Perhaps Alaine *had* shared details with her family. But then, why did her mother look at him with such open disgust? A king with no kingdom was hardly noteworthy, but neither did he deserve such derision for breaking up an unwanted marriage.

"Sir, I have gone to great lengths to be here today. I swear on my honor, I have uncovered the truth about your so-called debts and I can assure you, those loans were fabricated to deceive you and your family. The Magistrate is gathering evidence against Lord Baxter as we speak." Daric spoke to Mr. Martan directly, sincerity transforming his nervous ramblings into something vaguely coherent. "With all due respect, this man is not fit to wed your daughter. I love Alaine and I would see her make her own choice with regard to who she marries. She deserves as much."

Daric beamed at Alaine and she radiated gratitude in return. He would swear the clouds parted at that moment, revealing a hazy winter sun angled just so to shine upon them both.

"I couldn't agree more, ah—" Alaine's father trailed off for Daric to provide his name.

For the first time in many years, he called up the memory of his full name. "I am Prince Daric Astin Verril Halverson, though I no longer claim the title. I believe you may have heard of me. It would seem I am referred to as the—"

"The Lost Prince," said Baxter, the words slipping out of their own accord as his mouth hung agape. Recovering quickly, he snapped his mouth shut. "And I'm the heir apparent," he said, rolling his eyes. Though sarcasm coated his tongue, it could not mask the fear beneath. "You have proof of this claim?"

"He bears the Verril crest." Alaine's father pointed to his signet ring, the one item he still possessed of his past life.

"Any common thief can steal a ring. It does not verify your wild assertions." Oil coated Baxter's words as he sneered at no one in particular.

Daric fiddled with his ring absently, its solid weight a constant reminder of what he gave up to find love—to find Alaine. "As I said, I have no claim to that title, nor any ambition to see myself reinstated, but it is nevertheless who I am. I did not come here to deceive, but rather to shed light on the truth of this situation. The Martans should know the duplicity of the deal you made with them."

Baxter spluttered in the wake of the accusation. "I have never spoken falsely in my entire life. These allegations are unfounded and outrageous."

"Tell that to the Magistrate."

Daric exhaled in relief as a disembodied voice announced the arrival of Eudora.

Her fiery hair shone from a shadowed alcove by the entry, the perfect complement to the fierce expression revealed when she stepped into the light. On her heels came the Magistrate, wooden cane tapping out the rhythm of every other step. He was followed closely by the two guards from earlier, both with a firm grip on their weapons, looking like they would rather be any place else.

"Hi. I'm Eudora." The witch smiled brightly as she shook hands with the Martans, her confidence smoothing over the tension caused by Daric's brusqueness. She placed her arm around Alaine's mother's shoulders and gently guided her away from the group. Daric heard Eudora's quick, whispered words as they passed. "If you do anything to keep my girl from getting her happy ever after, I'll turn you into a stray cat—and not a cute one. One of those mangy, flea-bitten ones with one eye and half a tail."

She accentuated her promise with a small show of sparks shooting out from her fingertips, a wicked gleam in her eyes. Alaine let out a surprised chuckle even as her mother paled and touched a hand to her chest.

The tapping finally ceased as the Magistrate reached them, his breathing labored after the short walk from his office.

"Go ahead, Maggie," called Eudora. "Let them know what you found."

The older man looked up sharply at the nickname, but let it pass without reprimand as he caught his breath. With a shaking hand, he pulled a pair of spectacles from his pocket, placing them carefully upon his nose and ears before retrieving a folded slip of paper from another pocket.

"Lord Baxter, Mr. Martan." The Magistrate nodded his head to both men respectfully and squinted to read off his paper. "It has come to my attention that the circumstances surrounding a certain loan of the late Mr. Martan have been called into question. As such, I have scoured the documents at my disposal as Magistrate of Maribonne and representative of both the Baxters and the Martans."

Alaine danced from foot to foot, swaying in and out of Daric's periphery. His hands itched to reach for her, but he kept them firmly clenched at his sides, prepared to take on Baxter if it came to blows.

"I have found," continued the Magistrate, "that not only is there no evidence of the sum ever being transferred to the late Mr. Martan, but the only documentation I can find referencing such a loan appears to have been created post-mortem, by none other than Lord Baxter himself."

CHAPTER 45

Alaine

S he heard the words.

Heard them and understood what they meant—that she was free—but her body refused to respond to the joy she felt in her heart. Rather, she watched the next few moments unfold in slow motion like an outsider looking in.

Her mother collapsed. Her father, engrossed in conversation with the Magistrate, failed to notice that his wife was no longer vertical. To his credit, the Magistrate looked only slightly put off by the barrage of questions from her father. The two guards that had accompanied the Magistrate stood slightly off to the side. Though they no longer looked poised to draw arms, they watched the unfolding events with apparent trepidation, likely unsure how to proceed without orders.

Daric clapped Eudora on the back and she smiled over her shoulder at him. They looked for all the world like two old friends celebrating a victory. Alaine wondered how she had ever thought there was something more between them.

When Eudora stooped to attend to Alaine's mother, who showed no signs of movement beyond the slight rise and fall of her chest, Daric turned, slowly scanning the chaos that had erupted. Alaine waited for his eyes to sweep over her like the clouds parting to reveal the sun. Closing her eyes in anticipation, she loosed a breath, letting go of all the stress and pain of the past weeks. She felt the gentle caress of Daric's gaze and breathed in the sweet scent of a fresh start. Her smile crinkled the corners of her eyes as they fluttered open and focused instantly on Daric.

Daric's answering smile faltered and slipped as she felt his stare pass over her shoulder. His eyes widened, lips forming the shape of her name as two thickly muscled arms circled her.

Alaine knew, without seeing, that it was Baxter's arms wrapped around her, one at her neck, the other at her middle. She shuddered in response to his warm breath crawling along the back of her neck. Pressed tight against him, she instantly noted the difference between Baxter and Daric. The places where she molded so perfectly to Daric became angles that refused to align with Baxter's.

She struggled in his grasp, twisting and bucking in an attempt to loosen his hold on her, but he only squeezed tighter. The arm around her neck threatened her airways and she halted her futile attempts to escape.

A flicker of motion in her periphery made her realize the room had descended into perfect stillness, the people around her all but statues. All except Daric, who took another step toward her and her captor.

Baxter, having also noticed Daric's approach, whipped Alaine around, positioning her between the two men. She stumbled, nearly losing her footing but for the solid grip holding her upright. With her past behind her, literally holding her hostage, the future she yearned for remained just out of reach. She nearly came undone at the fear in Daric's face as he pulled free his blade.

"Release her, or I will kill you where you stand." The bravado in his voice masked the worry in his eyes, the promise of violence curling around the edges of his words.

Alaine couldn't see the guards, but she heard the clamor of their approach.

"Did you know," said Baxter without a hint of concern, "that you can kill a person with a sharp twist of their neck?" As if to emphasize his point, his fingers crept up her neck to cup her jaw. The gesture might have appeared innocuous—affectionate, even—to anyone who couldn't feel the fragile restraint he had on the anger within.

The sound of the guard's footsteps halted. Even Daric paused his attack as though weighing his chances. He had to consider that it had been hundreds of years since he'd last fought another person. Alaine knew the odds were stacked against him, knew also that he wouldn't risk her life. She saw the moment he decided to stand down and offered him a small smile of understanding.

"We had a deal," Baxter hissed in her ear.

She twisted her head away, wishing she could wipe away the feel of his breath on her ear. "It would seem, Lord Baxter, that if you want to hold to our deal, you owe my family a very large sum of money." She thought she had him. Surely she wasn't worth such a cost.

Baxter laughed, a joyless, hollow sound. "You want money? I'll give you money. You'll certainly not get any from your lost prince over there."

A muscle in Daric's jaw feathered, but he remained silent, leaving her to fight her own battle unless she called on him.

"I would rather have nothing than be married to you and have all the wealth in the world." She smiled despite her current predicament. This was not a battle she would allow Baxter to win.

"If it is nothing you want, it is nothing you shall get," he snarled. "I'll take everything you ever had, starting with your beauty, so that no other man shall be ensnared by your temptation."

The hand around her middle disappeared and she redoubled her escape efforts, twisting her hips and clawing at the arm that still held her. Though her efforts earned her a roar from Baxter, his grip on her did not falter. Spots danced in her vision and she kicked out with her feet, scrabbling for purchase as she fought for air.

The sound of a blade sliding free of its sheath was too near to be that of Daric's or the guards. She froze and felt her panic rising as Baxter pressed a dagger to the skin of her cheek. The cold steel glinted a hairsbreadth below her eye, candlelight reflecting off the polished surface.

Daric shouted something, his words incoherent around the sound of her heartbeat in her ears. She tried to call out to him, but her lungs refused to supply enough air to give voice to her words. Her panting gasps turned to silent sobs as he pressed the knife harder into her skin. She couldn't be sure if blood or tears leaked down her face, but she did know that she was done being the victim.

CHAPTER 46

Daric

Daric knew the moment Baxter abandoned reason. Blood trickled down Alaine's cheek from the knife he'd pulled on her—on the woman he claimed to desire, the woman he came to *marry* today. Already Daric's blood sang with all the wicked things he wanted to do in retaliation, but he bided his time for the sake of Alaine, for the sake of her precious light that didn't deserve to be extinguished.

The Magistrate was useless, Alaine's father little better, though at least he had the decency to stand between his fallen wife and the madman that held their daughter at knifepoint.

The guards at Baxter's back were his best bet, but even they hesitated at the risk to Alaine. Daric cocked his head to the side, catching the gaze of the closest guard and signaling to spread out with a subtle flick of his wrist.

With Baxter's focus completely on Alaine, the two guards crept closer, hands on their sword pommels, prepared to draw. Daric held his ground, but bent his knees, shifting his weight into his toes. He wanted to be prepared to spring for Alaine as soon as the guards attacked.

As if sensing the danger at his back, Baxter bared his teeth. Daric saw the muscles in his arm tense as he prepared to strike his final blow.

Pulling his blade free from the sheath at his hip, Daric lunged. He held his blade high, ready to plunge into Baxter and damn whatever consequences if it meant freeing Alaine.

At the last moment, he banked sideways, barely missing Eudora as she appeared seemingly from thin air. He staggered several steps until he regained his footing and watched mutely as the witch approached Alaine and her captor with naught but a single rose in her outstretched hand.

Baxter eyed Eudora warily, shoving the blade beneath Alaine's chin. Her throat bobbed against the cutting edge. Though she closed her eyes against the mounting horrors, she did not cry out.

"What do you think you're doing?" His words were for the witch, but he continued to monitor Daric and the guards, bracing for another attack.

With the knife now threatening her life, Daric was loath to move against him. A small head shake had the guards standing down as well. They wouldn't risk killing her in the process of apprehending Baxter.

"A gift, for the bride," said Eudora cryptically.

Baxter tensed, hackles raised at the perceived threat as her tentative steps brought her closer. The world held its breath as the witch paused mid-stride, the rose a mere handbreadth from kissing the knife at Alaine's throat.

"It is but a rose, my lord. What is it you fear from a simple flower? Its beauty? The fragility of its transient existence that begs it to be plucked before it decays? Or perhaps it is the thorns that trouble you. How dare the rose protect itself from those who seek to claim its beauty as their own."

Slowly, as though unconscious of his movements, Baxter lowered the knife. It was not enough to free herself, but Alaine shuddered at the reprieve. She exhaled slowly through her mouth, careful to keep her body as far from the blade as possible.

Baxter chuckled, a dark, mirthless laugh as he lifted his chin in indignation. "I am not afraid of a rose, you fool."

Eudora dared yet another step forward, lowering the rose as though handing it to Alaine. It disappeared from Daric's view as it dipped below her shoulders and he fought the desire to reposition himself.

"Then you won't mind me giving this one to Ms. Martan." It wasn't a question and Eudora didn't wait for Baxter's response before her arm shot forward.

Alaine's eyes flicked to him over Eudora's shoulder, equal parts bravery and fear reflected in their dark depths.

Eudora quickly backed away and Daric could see the rose now clutched in Baxter's hand where the knife had been. He hissed, dropping the rose and releasing Alaine to inspect his hand. The rose fell to the floor, blood glinting off its needle-sharp thorns as Alaine raised her hands to reveal the knife.

CHAPTER 47

Alaine

Alaine blinked and she was free. Baxter's hands fell away and she stumbled as she suddenly regained control of her limbs. She glanced down to her hands, the very ones that had taken the rose offered by Eudora, but rather than a flower, her hands now held a large dagger, the tip coated in blood where it had sliced her cheek.

Her initial reaction was to drop the offending blade, but she tightened her grip, whirling on Baxter as he blinked at his open palm. She held the dagger up with both hands, grateful they didn't shake when he looked up and realized what had become of his only weapon.

He raised his hands in supplication, but she gestured for the guards to take hold of him. They made quick work of securing his hands behind his back.

"Alaine—" he started, but she cut him off, sick of everything about him.

"No. You don't get to speak to me. If you want to live, you're going to listen, because I'm willing to bet that everyone here would look the other way if I sought retribution for everything you've done to me." Baxter cast a pleading glance around, but

Alaine heard no objections, unwilling to move her eyes away to confirm.

"I am not, nor will I ever be, yours. I am not a prize to be won, and your manhood—" she looked down pointedly, "does not entitle you to take whatever you please. Your obsession with beauty will be your undoing. Your inane quest for possession of it will yield you no fruit. The joy you feel will be as temporary as my beauty, your satisfaction as fleeting as spring. I have lived without my beauty, Henrik, and it is not so terrible a thing. But a life without love?" She shook her head and felt the gentle caress of Daric's gaze as it washed over her like a warm breeze. "That is the true tragedy. You will pay for your crimes against me and my family. Perhaps in doing so, you will find yourself humbled enough to treasure life's true values. Frankly, I don't care what happens to you. I'm going to walk out that door with the man that I love and never think of you again."

Alaine nodded to the taller guard, who began to haul Baxter away. He called after her, pleading for forgiveness and repeatedly proclaiming his namesake. His shouts echoed in the vaulted room until the three men disappeared through the arched doorway.

The knife slipped from her hands and clattered as it landed on the stone floor.

When strong arms again engulfed her, she didn't feel any spike in anxiety. She breathed in the comforting scent of pine and turned to press her face to Daric's chest, the emotions of the day overtaking her instantly. He rubbed circles on her back and whispered sweet nothings in her ear. The tone of his voice did more to calm her than the words themselves, of which she heard very little over her own sobs.

It occurred to her that she had never cried so much in her entire life.

When she came back to herself enough to feel the stares upon her, Alaine turned to face their awaiting audience.

Eudora waited patiently beside them, hands clasped in front of her mouth as her eyes welled with happy tears. A mirror smile appeared on Alaine's face as she embraced the young witch, all past misdeeds forgotten in the afterglow of victory.

"Thank you," Alaine whispered into Eudora's fiery curls.

They pulled apart, Eudora taking firm hold of Alaine's shoulders, every trace of sadness erased from her features. "It was the least I could do, after everything."

Alaine flinched as Eudora's fingers brushed against her injuries, an itching sensation following in their wake as her skin knit together.

"I left you a battle scar," said Eudora, pointing to her own unmarked cheek.

Alaine gave her a knowing glance, a grateful smile tugging at her lips.

A throat cleared to her right and Alaine turned to see her parents standing side by side. Her mother looked like a shell of the woman who had burst into her room that morning, pale and drawn like the rug had been pulled out from under her. Alaine got the sense that her mother was experiencing the disappointing failure of a long-held desire, but she couldn't dredge up an ounce of pity for the woman that birthed her. She was through pretending there was anything but blood between them.

On the other hand, her father beamed with pride and she felt her heart swell at his reaction, knowing she stood before him with no mask, only her true self bared for all to see.

It felt good to be free from not only Baxter but also society's constraints, from the expectations that she'd had to conform to from a young age.

She reached behind her, taking hold of Daric's hand and pulling him next to her. "Father, this is Daric." As she looked up at the man who held her heart, she sensed a culmination like a key sliding into its lock, like all her pieces had finally aligned and found their match in him. "And I love him."

The truth of those words rang throughout the room answered only by Daric's quiet, "And I her."

Her chest ached from the sheer magnitude of her joy and she knew that the happiness they shared was only amplified by the pain they had both endured to get here.

"That is plain for all to see." Her father stepped forward and clapped Daric heartily on the back.

"Well, then, are the two of you getting married today?"

In all the excitement that had unfolded, she'd forgotten about the poor officiant who'd gotten caught in the middle. The look on the officiant's face betrayed none of the fear or nerves she'd expect from someone who had witnessed all he had. Rather, he seemed curious, if not a little bored now that the thrill had passed.

She looked to Daric, not surprised at all to find him already looking at her. He chuckled as she lifted her eyebrows in question.

"Are you proposing to me?" Daric asked, his teasing smile softening the burn of the blush that colored her cheeks. "Of course I will marry you, Alaine, but it is your choice. It will always be your choice."

"Then, I'd like to wait." She only noticed the flicker of disappointment because she knew him so well, but she hurried on before he could respond. "Today is not the day for a wedding, not with blood crusting my dress and the gloom of winter presiding over us. I want—" she paused considering. "I want the roses to be in bloom when we marry. I want the sun on my face and birdsong in the air. And at the end of it all, when you are my husband and I am your wife, the shadows of our past shall be outshined by the brightness of our future together."

He smiled and pulled her close. "That sounds perfect," he whispered and captured her lips in a kiss that made her eager for the coming thaw.

Spring could not arrive soon enough.

CHAPTER 48

Epilogue

A t the height of spring, when the jasmine-scented breeze replaced the biting winter wind, Alaine and Daric married in an intimate ceremony with little fanfare. The sun shone brightly, illuminating her crown of roses as birds sang of their blessed union.

That evening, as the stars winked into existence, they bid farewell to Alaine's childhood hometown and walked into the forest, following the witch that had brought them together. Hand in hand, they traveled through magic to a place that would once again become their home.

The cottage looked no different on the outside than it had when Daric first stepped foot there hundreds of years prior, though Eudora took pains to remind them multiple times that the magic imbuing it had been broken with their curse.

"It is how you left it," she said as they stood before the door. "But so it shall remain. There will be no more instant breakfast or added rooms. That is, unless you do the labor yourselves." She winked and gathered them both in an embrace. Her eyes held unshed tears when they separated.

"I think I might miss you, witch," Daric said fondly.

"Don't worry. I'll be around." With that final cryptic message, she turned and disappeared into the trees, her red hair the last to fade into the dark.

For the first time in what felt like months, Alaine and Daric were alone at last. He wasted no time scooping her into his arms and carrying her through the doorway as she succumbed to a fit of giggles.

The air inside was stagnant—musty—something it had never been when it was under magical influence. He stalked to the hearth and deposited her gently on the sofa where they had spent many late nights immersed in conversation. Alaine ran her fingers over the fabric reverently as though sensing the memories held between the fibers.

"Cottage, a fire, if you please." Daric waited, but nothing happened, just as Eudora had said. Alaine gave him a wry look from the sofa. "What? It was worth a shot."

He was grateful for the time he'd spent in Alaine's village the past winter. Without it, he might have struggled in the sudden absence of magic. As it was, he was able to light a fire in a matter of moments, the heat quickly chasing off the lingering chill.

He rose and took a seat on the sofa next to Alaine. The seat groaned as it accepted his weight and Alaine tumbled into him, laying her head against his shoulder as he tucked her in close.

"Welcome home, my love," she murmured.

In the more than three hundred years Daric had been cursed, he'd never once considered the cottage his home. Here, now, with Alaine by his side, as much his as she was her own, the word felt right. This was their home because *she* was his home.

"You are sure you will be happy here so far from everyone you know?" Her relationship with her family had remained strained even following Baxter's trial and sentencing, but he needed to know that this was what she wanted. That she chose this life.

"I could not be happier to spend the rest of my life here with you." In her eyes, he saw the truth—the promise that this choice was the right choice.

"Welcome home, Alaine."

Acknowledgments

Despite having written an entire book, I'm actually not great with words. For evidence of this statement please continue reading this section. Additionally, I'd like to apologize in advance to anyone I may have forgotten to mention who was vital to the completion of this novel.

If I'm starting at the beginning, I have to thank my parents for always supporting me in whatever endeavors I pursue. Thank you, mom, for being the first to read everything I write. You showed me the power of hard work and convinced me that I may have some talent behind this passion of mine. To my dad, who was struck speechless when he learned I was publishing a book. You have always believed that I could do anything I set my mind to. Thank you for giving me the space to become my own person and for constantly encouraging my creativity.

Thank you to Meg, Reina, and Jess. As my late-night writing crew, you guys are the reason this book isn't sitting half-finished on my hard drive like my other three. I am eternally grateful for your endless advice and support.

Thank you to Cass, Selina, Bae, and Nisha for not only inspiring me to self-publish but also showing me the way. You're all #goals and I'm so grateful to know you.

Colby, you deserve extra thanks for reading this story when it was barely an idea and seeing the novel it could be. Without your guidance, who knows where Alaine and Daric would have ended up? You've been my biggest cheerleader throughout this entire process and your little editing notes gave me life. Thank you for turning my story into the best version of itself.

Jessica, your editing and launch assistance has been invaluable. I'm so grateful to have happened upon your services and hope that this isn't the end of our journey working together.

To all my platypi: Dee, Tiff, Chani, and those mentioned above, *none* of this would be possible if we hadn't banded together during NaNoWriMo of 2020. Even though this isn't the book I wrote with one hand while holding a month-old infant, the habits we started that month lead to the success of this book. In two and a half years, you have become some of my closest friends. It brings me so much joy to see us crushing our goals and doing all the things. You're all badasses and I'm so glad to have you in my life.

To aspiring writers out there, I encourage you to find your people. Surround yourself with those who will lift you up and inspire your creativity.

Thank you to my launch team and street team members. Your excitement for this book has given me the confidence needed to hit the publish button. I appreciate all you've done to get the word out about my little debut.

Thank you to my readers for taking a chance on an indie debut, whether you know me personally or not. Your support means the world to me.

And finally, thank you to my husband for thinking I'm *neat* and buying my book even though you'll never read it. You are the Daric to my Alaine (which I realize means nothing to you since you don't read) and I love you so much. I figure if there's a chance of you reading any part of this book, maybe it will be the last paragraph.

About the Author

Elle Backenstoe lives in Eastern Pennsylvania with her husband, son, and two dogs. She grew up with her nose buried in a book and sometimes emerges long enough to write some words of her own. She writes fantasy and romance, often together. Elle runs on pop punk music and Coke, and will always choose sweet over salty. When she's not reading or writing, you can find her at her home-away-from-home, the dance studio.

Follow Elle on social media:
Instagram: @ellebackenstoewrites
Twitter: @ellebackenstoe
TikTok: @ellebackenstoe
Facebook: www.facebook.com/ellebackenstoe

For the latest news and updates regarding upcoming books by Elle, sign up for her newsletter at https://www.ellebackens toe.com